Acclaim for Ha Jin*'s*

In the Pond

"Fascinating, refreshing, and uncommonly subtle: Ha Jin has made China available to a new world and a world of new readers." —*Kirkus Reviews*

"Ha Jin's account of life in China reminds us both of the universality of human folly and of the immense, perverse pleasure to be found in its representation. *In the Pond* is more than a fun read, it is that great delight, a profoundly humorous book. As art confronts politics in memorably undignified fashion, we laugh while we wince, admiring between gasps the steady control of the writing." —Gish Jen, author of *Who's Irish?*

"Ha Jin's Dismount Fort teems with vivid life and people who grow ever less strange as the struggles unfold. An exotic subject matter helps, but narrative talent proves victorious." —*Time*

"Ha Jin's first novel entirely fulfills the promise of his stunning stories—opening for the western reader a world that until now has been barely imaginable or imagined. Ha Jin's sure prose, his deft characterization, his wit, and above all his compassion together tear down the global wall. A reader can only thank him."

—James Carroll, author of *An American Requiem*

"*In the Pond* is a superbly readable, funny and moving fable about the power of art to dispel dark forces within and without. Ha Jin's rapidly flowering mastery of storytelling in English is one of the wonders of contemporary American literature."

—Ralph Lombreglia, author of *Make Me Work*

Ha Jin

In the Pond

Ha Jin left his native China in 1985 to attend Brandeis University. He is the author of the internationally bestselling novel *Waiting,* which won the PEN/Faulkner Award and the National Book Award; the story collections *The Bridegroom,* which won the Asian American Literary Award and the Townsend Prize for Fiction, *Under the Red Flag,* which won the Flannery O'Connor Award for Short Fiction, and *Ocean of Words,* which won the PEN/Hemingway Award; the novels *The Crazed* and *War Trash*; and three books of poetry. He lives in the Boston area and is a professor of English at Boston University.

ALSO BY HA JIN

Fiction

Under the Red Flag
Ocean of Words
Waiting
The Bridegroom
The Crazed
War Trash

Poetry

Between Silences
Facing Shadows
Wreckage

In the Pond

A Novel

Ha Jin

VINTAGE INTERNATIONAL
Vintage Books
A Division of Random House, Inc.
New York

FIRST VINTAGE INTERNATIONAL EDITION, MAY 2000

 Published in the United States by Vintage Books, a division of Random House, Inc., New York, and simultaneously in Canada by Random House of Canada Limited, Toronto. Originally published in hardcover in the United States by Zoland Books, Inc., Cambridge, Massachusetts, in 1998.

Library of Congress Cataloging-in-Publication Data on file.

Vintage ISBN: 0-375-70911-8

www.vintagebooks.com

Printed in the United States of America
10 9 8

for Wen

Alas, after all's been said, I still can't choose a virtuous man as my hero. I can explain why: the virtuous man has been turned into a sort of horse and there's no author who hasn't ridden him, urging him on with his whip or whatever comes to hand. Now I feel the time has come to make use of a rogue. So let's harness him for a change!

—NIKOLAI GOGOL
Dead Souls

In the Pond

One

SHAO BIN FELT SICK of Dismount Fort, a commune town where he had lived for over six years. His wife, Meilan, complained that she had to walk two miles to wash clothes on weekends. She couldn't pedal, so Bin was supposed to take her on the carrier of his bicycle to the Blue Brook. But this month he worked weekends in the Harvest Fertilizer Plant and couldn't help her. If only they had lived in Workers' Park, the plant's apartment compound, which was just hundreds of paces away from the waterside. These days Meilan prayed to Buddha at night, begging him to help her family get an apartment in the park soon.

"Don't worry. We'll have one this time," Bin told her Wednesday afternoon.

"How can you be so sure?"

"They should give us one. I have more seniority than others."

"That can't be a guarantee."

Indeed he had worked in the plant for six years. According to the principle of need and seniority, this time it seemed the Shaos should have a new apartment, but Meilan was not optimistic. "You know," she said, "if I were you I'd give Secretary Liu and Director Ma two bottles of Grain Sap each. I heard that lots of people have visited them in the evenings. You shouldn't just sit and wait."

"Forget it. I won't spend any money on them."

"Stubborn ass," she said under her breath.

Bin was a small man. He used to be healthy and stout, but in recent years he had lost so much weight that people called him Skeleton behind his back. Despite his physique, he was both talented and arrogant. He was better read than others in the plant, and he knew a lot of ancient stories, even the adventures of Sherlock Holmes. What is more, his handwriting was handsome. That was why some women workers used to say to one another, "If only the man was as good looking as his handwriting." When he was engaged to Meilan five years before, people had been amazed and remarked, "A beauty loves a scholar indeed." Although Meilan was not beautiful and Bin was not a true scholar, compared with him she was a better match, having several suitors.

Since they were married, they had lived in one room in a dormitory house on Old Folk Road, owned by Meilan's work unit, the People's Department Store. They now had a lively two-year-old, for whom alone the room, twelve feet by twenty, was hardly enough. Besides, Bin was an amateur painter and calligrapher, though officially he was a fitter. As an artist, he needed space, ideally a room for himself, where he could cultivate and practice his art, but that had been impossible. Every night he stayed up late, wielding a writing brush with the table lamp on, which disturbed his wife's and baby's sleep. And the room was always saturated with an inky smell. Often Meilan had to open the windows in the cold winter, yet Bin had no other way to do brushwork. How the Shaos were longing for decent housing.

These days Bin had been trying in vain to find out whether or not his name was on the list being considered by the Housing Committee. Most of his fellow workers grew reticent and mysterious, as though all of a sudden everybody had struck gold; they became mean to others.

Now it's my turn to have an apartment, Bin repeated to himself on Thursday morning, when he was repairing a hydraulic jack for the Transport Team. The night before, Meilan's words about the workers' bribing the leaders had sown some fear in him; yet he kept reminding himself not to lose heart.

Sooner than he expected, in the afternoon the final list was posted on the notice board at the plant's front entrance. Bin went there but didn't find his name among the lucky ones. He was outraged; so were many others. In all the workshops angry voices were rising while those who had been assigned apartments turned silent at once. Some workers said they would put out big-character posters without delay, to expose the leaders' corruption. A few declared they were going to demolish the four larger apartments built for the leaders, blowing them up with packages of TNT at night. But this was merely bluff; the same thing had been said many times before, and nothing of the sort had ever taken place here.

As soon as the electric bell announced the end of the shift, Bin left the plant. He was cycling home absently, an army cap askew on his head and his white shirt unbuttoned, its tail flapping gently behind him. His mind was full. How should he break the bad news to Meilan? She would be so disappointed. How could he console her?

The moment he passed the railroad crossing near the northern end of the plant, he saw the Party secretary, Liu Shu, walking ahead with his hands clasped behind. Bin caught up with him and got off his bicycle. "May I have a word with you, Secretary Liu?" he said.

"All right." Liu stopped and straightened up a little, his hooded eyes half closed.

"Why didn't I get housing this time?" Bin asked.

"You're not alone. Over a hundred comrades are still in line. Don't you know that?"

"I've worked in our plant for six years. Hou Nina has been here for only three years, but she got an apartment this time. Why? I cannot understand this."

Liu told him bluntly, "That's a decision made by the Housing Committee. They believe she needs it more than you. Women and men are equal in our new society. You have a place to live now, but she has stayed with her folks in the village all these years. She needs her own place to get married. Her wedding has been put off twice; she can't remain single forever."

Bin wanted to yell: She can live with you, can't she? But he didn't say a word; instead, he turned and hopped on his National Defense bicycle, riding away without saying good-bye to the secretary. He couldn't help cursing Liu to himself, "Son of a tortoise, you've had a good apartment already, but you took a larger one this time. You've abused your power. This is unfair, unfair!"

The stocky secretary shook his head and said to Bin's back, "Idiot!"

Bin planned to break the bad news to his wife after dinner, but seeing his dark face, Meilan sensed that something was wrong and asked him several times what it was. He went ahead and told her; he even mentioned that Hou Nina, the junior accountant, had received a new apartment. At this, tears came to Meilan's eyes, and she cursed the leaders loudly. She also blamed Bin for his stubbornness, saying, "A few bottles of liquor are a small cost. How many times did I tell you? But you wouldn't listen."

"Come and eat," he said, picked up a pair of chopsticks, and lifted a bowl of noodles to his mouth, slurping the soup. Then with a spoon he put some minced toon leaves into his bowl.

"I don't want to eat, I'm full of gas." She turned and pushed the window open. Outside, a breeze passed by and shook a few raindrops off the aspen leaves, pattering through the trees. A frog was croaking hesitantly.

"What are you going to do?" she asked.

"I don't know. What do you think?"

"They've maltreated us. You should report those corrupt men."

Bin didn't answer and went on eating. Shanshan, their baby daughter, was stirring her bowl of custard with a green plastic spoon, waiting for her mother to feed her. A short noodle was lying on her white bib, near the red bill of an embroidered dove.

Meilan, in a sky blue dress, remained at the window, her shapely chest bulging a little as she was still fuming. She raised her hand and put a strand of hair back behind her small ear; she leaned over the sill and spat out the window. Once in a while she wiped the tears off her cheeks with her thumb and forefinger.

After dinner Bin was sitting outside the dormitory house, smoking and waving a fan on which spread a misty landscape — a temple, a river, and two slender boats, each punted by a tiny fisherman in a straw hat. His Adam's apple moved up and down while his lean face looked tense. He was deep in thought; his small eyes narrowed as the bushy brows joined. Above his head flared a 25-watt lightbulb, around which a puff of gnats were flitting, a few mosquitoes buzzing among them. The air smelled of rotten fish and fresh corn. Beyond the high wall two trucks were tooting their horns on the street, as if quarreling.

In the middle of the courtyard, Meilan was washing bowls and dishes with an angry clatter at the faucet. Bin understood that this time he had been in the wrong. A wise man should do everything to preempt bad odds, as Meilan had told him, but he had been impervious to reason and let the bad odds multiply. Unlike his plant, the department store had only sixteen employees; it was unable to build an apartment house on its own. So his family depended on him to get decent housing, but he had blown the opportunity. Who could tell in what year a new apartment would be available again? Heaven knew how long his family would have to live in this single room.

Choking with anger, he was determined to do something about the injustice. Even though he couldn't correct the leaders' wrongdoing, he wanted to teach them an unforgettable lesson and show them that he wouldn't swallow an offense. But what should he do?

He remembered that the materialist thinker Wang Chong of the Han Dynasty had said something about punishing the evil with the writing brush. He couldn't recall the exact words. That passage must have been in the paperback *The Essence of Ancient Chinese Thought,* which he had read a few weeks before. He stood up and went back into the room. On the top of a wicker bookshelf, the book was sandwiched between an epigraphic dictionary and an album of flower paintings. He pulled it out and without difficulty found the passage, since he had folded the bottom corner of the page as a bookmark. He perused Wang Chong's words:

> How can writing be merely playing with ink and toying with brush? It must record people's deeds and bequeath their names to posterity. The virtuous hope to have their deeds remembered and therefore exert themselves to do more good; the wicked fear having their doings recorded and therefore make efforts to restrain themselves. In brief, the true scholar's brush must encourage good and warn against evil.

Bin closed the book, profoundly moved. Writing and painting belong to the same family of arts, he reasoned; they are both the work of the brush. Yes, to fight the evil is the essential function of fine arts. As an artist and scholar I ought to expose those corrupt leaders. Whatever they are, painting and writing must not be embroidery and decoration; they must have strength and a soul — a healthy, upright spirit. A good piece of work should be as lethal as a dagger to evildoers.

After Meilan and Shanshan went to bed, Bin began

grinding an ink stick in his antique ink slab, which was in the shape of a crab, carved out of a Gold Star stone. His hand kept moving clockwise in tiny circles. The ink was ready in a few minutes; he picked up a brush made of weasel's hair and began to draw a cartoon. On a large sheet of paper he drew a huge official seal, standing upside down. Then on the seal's bulky handle he sketched an ecstatic face with a few hairs on the crown. Up on the seal's flat top, which was in the form of an oval stage, he put a dozen midget men and women sitting together in two rows. He made sure that two of them in the center resembled Secretary Liu and Director Ma. Liu, wearing a handlebar mustache, sat with his short arms crossed before his chest, while Ma's long face was pulled downward as though his mouth was filled with food. Behind the human figures Bin set up a six-story building with broad balconies and tall windows, from which fluorescent rays were darting out.

The drawing finished, Bin dipped a smaller brush in the ink, then wrote a line of bold characters at the top of the paper as the title: "Happy Is the Family with Power."

The excitement of creating a meaningful piece of work kept him awake after he went to bed. He forced himself to count his heartbeats, which were faster than the second hand of the clock on the wall. His temples were tight, and his head wouldn't cool down; within two hours he got up three times to urinate in the outhouse in the west corner of the courtyard. Not until two o'clock did he go to sleep.

The next morning he showed the cartoon to his wife. "Good, good," she said. "I hope this will be a land mine and blast them."

Carefully he stuffed it into a manila envelope addressed to the *Lüda Daily*, a regional newspaper in which he had published three words of calligraphy. On his way to work, he went up Bank Street and dropped the envelope into the mailbox in front of the post office.

Two

FOR DAYS the whole plant was talking about the housing assignments. The leaders had anticipated the discontent and were not worried. Only two big-character posters, fewer than they had expected, appeared in the plant; both were pasted on the side wall of the office building. One was entitled "Workers' Park Is Not for the Workers to Inhabit"; the other, "What Makes the Housing Principle Flexible?"

Though the two posters touched on bribery and the privileges the leaders had granted themselves, Secretary Liu and Director Ma were not daunted by this sort of writing. What they feared was that some workers might put out posters at the Commune Administration, appealing to their superiors to interfere with the plant's housing, but so far nothing of that kind had happened. In fact, the workers' bitter voices were dwindling.

The mollification was mainly the result of four buckets of human excrement that had been secretly dumped into the larger apartments, one bucket in each. For two days the unused rooms stank and teemed with flies and maggots; some of the walls were soiled.

It was a simpleminded trick, far from reaching the effect the rumor claimed: the leaders would no longer want the stinking apartments. On the contrary, they still meant to move in, though it was true that Liu and Ma had been outraged and almost called an emergency meeting after seeing the mess. But both of them were seasoned cadres and hadn't acted rashly.

"We should report it to town police," Ma said to Liu, returning from the park.

"You really think so?"

"Yes, it's damage to public property, you know."

"Forget it, Old Ma. We've no idea where the shit came from or who to suspect. The police can't do a thing if we don't give them any clue."

"Then what should we do?"

After exchanging views, they decided to keep quiet about the incident and not have it investigated, because they felt that their reticence might pacify the workers some. Indeed it did; within a few days they could see that those resentful eyes became less hostile.

Director Ma assigned a group of temporary workers, hired from a nearby village, to clean and whitewash the walls of the apartments and scrub the cement floors with caustic soda and Lysol. The two leaders went to Workers' Park over ten times within a week to ensure that no trace of human stench was left in their future homes. Afterwards, their wives also went over to check the sanitary conditions. Mrs. Ma wanted the window frames and the doors to be repainted; this took four workers another day.

In three weeks the cartoon appeared in the literary and art section of the *Lüda Daily.* Apparently, the editors of the newspaper hadn't taken it as a significant piece of work; it came out only four by three inches, inserted in the bottom left corner of the page. Yet the author's name, authenticated by the mention of his workplace, stood below the drawing. Anyone with a little imagination wouldn't fail to link the happy crowd in the cartoon to the cadres of the Harvest Fertilizer Plant.

Though only a few people in the plant subscribed to the newspaper, more than half of the three hundred workers and staff saw or heard of the cartoon on the day of its publication. That night, someone even pasted a copy of it on the notice board at the front entrance. Because Bin was its author, people assumed he had sneaked to the plant at night and posted it there. In fact, he didn't know of its appearance in the newspaper until he came to work early the next morning.

On arriving at the plant, Bin was surprised to see his cartoon on the notice board. Several workers were gathered near it, chattering and smoking. They all congratulated him, but Bin nodded without showing any enthusiasm. In his heart he was happy and couldn't help thinking, Good, see how those bastards will patch up the whole thing. This will make them remember that I don't forget an offense in a hurry.

Entering the workshop, he ran into the director of Maintenance, Hsiao Peng, whose rank was not high enough to qualify him to compete for one of the four larger apartments; so Hsiao was among the outraged too. With a cunning smile he said to Bin, "That's not a bad drawing, Young Shao. I'm impressed."

"I aimed it at some people," Bin said, his jaw jutting out.

"I know, you mean to correct the unhealthy tendency in our plant." Hsiao was chewing a toffee, his round eyes blinking.

Bin knew Hsiao was also one of the wolves, who grumbled only because he hadn't got a piece of meat this time. Quietly he turned away to put on his work clothes.

Within an hour after the morning shift started, the cartoon disappeared from the board. In the director's office, Liu and Ma were restless, thinking how to handle this situation. Now they were notorious in the entire prefecture, only because they each had a faucet and an extra room in their new homes. Many leaders of higher authorities must have seen the cartoon and might have inquiries made about the people involved. That damn dog Shao Bin had turned upon his masters. No wonder people called him Man Hater. He simply hated everyone and couldn't bear to see anybody better off than himself. They had to figure out a way to subdue him now; otherwise some workers would follow his example and make more trouble for them.

That evening the plant held a workers-and-staff meeting in the dining hall. After everybody was seated, Secretary Liu began to speak about the allocation of cabbages, turnips, carrots, and rutabagas for the coming winter, and also about the coal that the plant would sell to its employees to supplement the fuel the state had rationed. After that, he turned to the main topic: the cartoon and its author. In a thick voice, the squat secretary announced that this was a serious political case and that Shao Bin, "a representative of bourgeois liberalism," had to be responsible for all the consequences.

Liu explained, "Comrade Shao Bin never expressed his dissatisfaction with the housing assignment. Then without the leaders' knowledge and permission, he sent the cartoon to the newspaper. This is a sniping attack. As a result, he has damaged our plant's reputation and slung mud in our faces. Besides, this is pure slander. You all know that only five single-story houses were built this year, but Shao Bin set up a tall building with his brush. In our commune no house is taller than White Mansion, which has only two stories. That's a fact. How could our plant own a six-story building? If Comrade Shao is so constructive, we'd better invite him to build us a few great mansions. Then everybody here will have a spacious, beautiful unit. That will solve the problem of our lack of funds. In a couple of weeks we'll realize the ideal of Communism in our plant, and we'll become a progressive model for all of China."

The audience laughed.

Liu went on, "In the cartoon twelve adults, men and women, are painted as one family; this is an insult to those who have moved into the new apartments. Everybody knows that many workers got housing this time. How dare Shao Bin call the twenty-four families that live in the new houses 'one family with power'? Comrades, we are not animals but human beings. We grew out of group marriage thousands of years ago. You know, only the reactionaries would say the Communists live together, sharing wives and husbands. In the old China I often heard that kind of propaganda on Chiang Kai-shek's radio. Perhaps Comrade Shao Bin is too young to know the malicious nature of his drawing, but obviously it has nothing to do with constructive criticism. If he was not full of reactionary intentions, he at least called us names."

Some angry eyes turned to Bin, who was sitting by a window. He hung his head low, dragging at a self-rolled cigarette.

"You want to say something, Old Ma?" Liu asked the director, returning to his seat.

"Yes." Ma went to the front and began speaking in a

hoarse voice. "Comrades, it's true that the larger apartments each have an extra room, but it was designed for work, not for comfort. Don't you think the leaders need a room to talk with you when you have a problem and come to see us? We can't discuss it at a dining table with women and kids around, can we? Besides, all the leaders have large families, you know that, and we need an extra room. This is not our fault. When we were young, the government encouraged us to make babies, the more the better, and there was no family planning at the time. Chairman Mao announced at a conference, 'Among all things in the world the most precious are human beings.' We responded to his call, making more babies to increase our national wealth." Some women giggled. Ma kept on, "So I say an extra room in our homes is not a privilege but a necessity."

Damn you! Bin cursed to himself. How about the faucet and the closets? How about taking the sunniest side of each house? How about the cement floors? I hope the hard floors will break your women's hips.

Ma then announced the Party Committee's decision about the cartoon. "In view of comrade Shao Bin's wrong, we propose a threefold solution here. One, Finance will stop giving him a bonus for six months. Two, he must write out a self-criticism and admit his wrong publicly, in front of all of us. Three, he must send a letter, without delay, to the *Lüda Daily* and explain the facts and his true intention, and ask the editors to publish a note of correction. Comrades, we believe this is the only way to restore our plant's reputation and repair the leader' image. Let me make it clear here: we will adopt other measures if Shao Bin doesn't change his attitude toward —"

"This is oppression and vengeance!" Bin bellowed and jumped up. "I won't write a word. I will report you to the State Council in Beijing." He flourished his cigarette.

The room rang with laughter. Ma waved to adjourn the meeting, and people stood up, moving to the door. Bin knew there was no use arguing with the leaders, who would simply enjoy seeing him rage and wrangle, so he left the dining hall without one more word. His eyes turned triangular, glowing with anger.

After hearing of the Party Committee's decision, Meilan changed her mind and begged her husband to give up confronting the leaders, because there was 120 yuan involved. The loss really hurt. Without the money, they wouldn't be able to buy a TV the next year. They had saved almost 300 yuan for that and needed the bonus to make up the total amount. But Bin refused to give in, saying he wouldn't have to watch television and he would rather spend his time more meaningfully, studying and painting. Besides, how could he retreat now? People would think him spineless if he bowed to the leaders' wishes.

However, the loss of the bonus also upset him. At the least it meant they would be hard up by New Year's. A self-criticism in front of the whole plant was out of the question; a letter to the newspaper would be impracticable as well. Apart from impairing his dignity, to retract what he had published would wreck his career as an artist, and he would be regarded as a liar by the editors of the newspapers and magazines with which he had connections. But if he didn't meet the demands announced by Director Ma, the leaders would surely have the bonus deducted from his pay. It was obvious he had no way to stop them from doing that, so he decided to let it be. What else could they do to him? Hardly anything. They couldn't fire him, because he was a permanent worker in a state enterprise and didn't have to renew his contract as a temporary worker would. As long as his job was secure, he shouldn't worry too much. Of course, from now on they would make things difficult for him, but he wasn't a soft egg, easy to crush.

Despite his tough reasoning, Bin regretted having sent out the cartoon that had cost him a sum larger than two months' wages. By contrast, from the *Lüda Daily* he had received only a Worker-Peasant fountain pen and a canvas satchel, which came in a parcel together with two copies of the newspaper. In all, they were worth about five yuan. If only Meilan had changed her mind and stopped him when she had seen the cartoon that morning. If only he had known of the price in advance. Too late now; it was impossible to recover the water thrown on the ground.

Now that he was already in the thick of the fight, he had best engage the enemy. The most effective strategy he could think of was to report them to the commune leaders. Yes, if the devil expanded a foot, the Buddha would grow a yard. He was going to expose the two petty officials, disgrace them, and have them investigated and punished by their superiors.

A strong sense of justice and civil duty rose in him. An upright man ought to plead in the name of the people. He believed he was going to voice not only his own discontent and indignation but also the oppressed brothers' and sisters'. Yes, he wanted to speak for all the workers in the plant.

For two weeks Bin put aside reading and painting and concentrated on writing a lengthy letter of accusation to Yang Chen, who was the Party secretary of the commune and Liu's and Ma's immediate superior. Though it didn't own the plant, the commune supervised it on behalf of the state. So Yang should be the first person with whom to lodge such an accusation. Every night Bin worked on the letter into the small hours.

Through many years' persevering effort, he had cultivated a scholarly habit — writing everything in brush, whether it was a title for his painting or a grocery list, unless he was pressed for time and had to resort to a pen. He had been extremely careful about his handwriting; according to the instructions of ancient masters, handwriting is something like the writer's looks. No, more than looks, it displays his taste, cultivation, respiratory rhythm, mental state, spiritual aspiration, manly strength, and, most important of all, his moral character. Once on paper, everything must be brilliant and dignified, even a dot. Therefore Bin had always been conscientious about his calligraphy.

As a budding calligrapher of sorts, he was patient, ambitious, and diligent. He enjoyed seeing his own words take shape on paper and loved the fragrance of his authentic ink stick, whose brand was always the same: Dearer Than Gold.

The letter of accusation was completed. All together it consisted of thirty pages, about eight thousand words, every one of which was written in the meticulous style of Little Flies. Bin listed the crimes committed by the two leaders in the past few years, including not giving him a raise the year before on the grounds that he hadn't shown enough respect for them; persecuting him because he was more artistic and creative than others; feasting at the plant's cost whenever an important visitor arrived (Secretary Liu had once got so drunk that he had wet both his pants and a sofa in the conference room); accepting a lot of bribes from the poor workers and staff; using the plant's trucks to transport coal, vegetables, furniture, bricks, and sand to their homes; allowing their wives to meddle with administrative affairs; at every Spring Festival, allotting themselves an extra sack of polished rice, ten pounds of peanut oil, a crate of liquor (sixteen bottles), a hamper of apples, a block of frozen ribbonfish (fifty pounds), and two large bundles of potato noodles.

Of course, the most atrocious crime they had perpetrated in the plant was to suppress different opinions and try to get rid of the dissidents. The letter concluded with these questions:

> Who are the masters of this plant? The workers or the two corrupt leaders? Where is their Communist conscience? Why are they more vicious and more avaricious than landowners and capitalists in the old China? Should they still remain in the Party? Are we, the common workers, supposed to trust the parasites like Liu Shu and Ma Gong? As a citizen of a great socialist country, do I still have the right to speak up for justice and democracy?

Bin had been wondering whether he should mention that there must have been an affair between Liu Shu and Hou Nina, but he was uncertain how to discuss the problem of Liu's lifestyle.

The summer before last, by chance he had seen Nina doing the splits in the secretary's office. One afternoon Bin went there to hand in his application for the Party membership. At the door he heard a female voice tittering inside, so he stopped to see what was happening. Through a crack in the door, he saw Nina spreading her legs on the floor; her body was sinking lower and lower while her lips bunched together as though she was in pain. Yet she was smiling, her eyes blinking. With her pink skirt wrapped around her waist, she put both hands on her thighs to force them to touch the floor. Bin thought Liu would move over and do something unusual — make a pass or pinch her thigh or hip, but the secretary didn't budge, merely chuckled and said, "Get up, girl. Don't hurt yourself. Enough." He was drinking tea and cracking spiced pumpkin seeds.

"See, see I still can do it!" she cried, her entire legs on the cement floor. Her chin was thrown up at Liu.

Bin knocked at the door, and without waiting he went in. His intrusion startled them; they both stood up.

"What do you want?" Liu asked.

"I came to hand in my application for Party membership, Secretary Liu." Bin put the writing on the desk.

"All right, I'll read it." Liu looked disconcerted.

Bin turned back to the door, giving Nina a long stare that revealed his knowledge of what had just happened. He went out without a word.

Now, Bin suspected Liu had probably been so mean to him because he had spoiled his luck with Nina that day. How he regretted that he had not witnessed the whole episode. If only he had waited outside a little longer to find out the true relationship between them. Then he would have possessed firsthand evidence. O Impatience, the enemy of any achievement, and the sin of sins. All he could do now was add a postscript to the accusation, saying he believed there must have been an affair between the two. He asked the superiors to investigate.

After breakfast the next morning, he sealed the letter and cycled to the Commune Administration at the corner of Bank and Main streets to deliver it personally, also to save postage. Secretary Yang hadn't arrived yet. After waiting ten minutes to no avail, Bin left the letter with Yang's aide, Dong Cai, a slim, middle-aged man with a toothy face, wearing a green sweater.

"Secretary Yang will read it as soon as he has time," Dong assured him with a grin, flicking the Grape cigarette Bin had given him.

"Thanks for the help. Thanks," Bin said with a bow.

Because of delivering the letter, he was one hour late for work that morning. But who cared? He felt he had done something more meaningful than maintaining machines.

Three

AFTER TWENTY-FOUR FAMILIES moved in, Workers' Park became livelier than before. A hot-water room was built near the entrance, and the two old guards were told to take care of the boiler. Hundreds of sycamore saplings were planted around the houses, to "green the park," as the leaders declared. For the children, a small soccer field was flattened out at the foot of the slope, near the bend of the Blue Brook. From now on, at seven in the morning, a truck would take the teenagers to the Fourth Middle School, which was three miles northeast of Dismount Fort, and it would bring them back at five in the afternoon. A few housewives proposed to open a grocery store in the compound; it was a good idea, supported by the workers and leaders. Things began to be systemized in the park, while those who lived outside grew more jealous.

The leaders promised that everybody would eventually move into the compound. There was enough land,

and what prevented them from having more houses built was the lack of funds. They urged the workers to be patient.

On Wednesday afternoon Bin went to Finance, which was in the basement of the office building, to pick up his wages. Nina was in a bad mood, because Director Ma had just told her to take charge of selling the tickets for hot water. From now on, the families living in Workers' Park would come to her to buy water tickets. It wasn't a lot of work, but to her mind, she shouldn't have to handle such a trifle, unrelated to accountancy. The old guards at the park could easily take care of the business. But she didn't complain in front of Ma; for the time being, she knew she ought to appear grateful to the leaders for giving her a new apartment.

At the sight of Bin, she asked, "Your pay?"

"Yes, please."

She pulled out a drawer, picked up a small envelope, and handed it to him. Bin noticed two dark bruises on her forearm; he had heard that her fiancé often beat her.

He wet his thumb and forefinger on his tongue and began counting the wages, while Nina resumed reading the magazine *Chinese Women.* To his surprise, there was only forty-two yuan, fifty fen less than his monthly pay; this meant he lost two pounds of beer or a dish of stewed pork. "Why did you give me half a yuan less after you took away my bonus?"

"*I* docked your bonus? You lost it yourself," she

said with sudden passion, her curved eyebrows going straight. "That half yuan was the haircut fee. Director Ma told me not to give you that."

"Why?"

"Don't know why. I was told to do so." She flicked her fingers at him, annoyed.

"If you don't know why, why did you do it?"

"Give me a break, all right?" She stared him in the face and put the magazine on her lap. "I'm busy, no time to listen to you talking like this. Go ask Director Ma yourself."

Feeling it useless to argue, Bin made for the door.

"Lunatic," Nina said under her breath.

"What did you say?" He turned back.

"Lunatic, lu-na-tic!" she cried out, stressing every syllable, then pursed her lips, glaring at him.

"You know, girl, you have a filthy mouth, but I don't want to clean it out for you. Don't want to dirty my hands."

"Go to hell. Only because you didn't get an apartment, you act like everybody owes you a thousand. Get out of here, lunatic."

"Bitch!"

"What did you call me?"

"I call you whore, a whore who's stripped in every office." He moved to the door.

"Stop! Get your ass back here."

Ignoring her, Bin went straight to the director's office

on the second floor. Ma and Liu were in a meeting with two other men, the chairman of the union, Hong Bao, and the secretary of the Communist Youth League, Huang Dongfang. At the sight of Bin's dark face, Liu and Ma stood up simultaneously.

Bin asked loudly why Ma had had his haircut fee deducted. Ma answered, "You were one hour late for work last Thursday, weren't you? It's our policy to be strict and fair in meting out rewards and punishments. This is our way of keeping discipline in the plant. You should look to yourself for an explanation before coming to me."

Bin realized he couldn't get the money back, so he changed his topic, reporting to the leaders that Accountant Hou Nina had called him a lunatic just now, in her office.

"You are a lunatic," Liu said matter-of-factly. "I believe so too."

"What?"

"Yes, we all think you have a mental disorder or something," Ma said, wiggling his forefinger at his temple. "You'd better go to the hospital and have your brain checked."

"What? You two are leaders. You must not insult me like this."

"Who insulted you?" Ma asked with a surprised look, then poked Bin in the chest with his fist.

"Why use your hand? I came to you for help, but instead of listening to me, you call me names and beat me."

"Who beat you?" Ma gave him a slap on the face.

"You, you're doing it now!"

Liu stepped forward and cuffed him on the neck, then asked with a smile, "Who beat you? Can you prove it? Who is your witness?" He clasped his hands behind him.

Bin, rubbing his neck, looked at Bao and Dongfang. They were sitting there quietly, their eyes fixed on the glass top of the table.

Ma pushed Bin to the door, shouting, "Get out of here, lunatic." He kicked him in the butt.

The door slammed shut and almost touched the tip of Bin's nose.

Bin heard Liu curse inside the office, "Such an idiot." He wanted to burst in, spring on the two leaders, and choke the breath out of them, but he was no match for them, especially Ma, who was tall and burly and had once been on a divisional basketball team in the People's Army. Besides, Liu wore new bluchers, which looked lethal.

Yet the rage was too much for Bin to hold down, so he yelled out, "I screw your ancestors! I screw them pair by pair!" He kicked the door and then hurried away.

He remembered that his father had once wanted him to learn kung fu from an old man in their home village and offered to pay the tuition for him. But Bin hadn't been interested and had spent his free time with the art teacher at the elementary school, learning how to paint.

Now, how he regretted that he hadn't followed his father's advice! Had he done that, he could have burst into the office and felled the two rabbits to the floor with the Eagle Palm.

Bin didn't want to have dinner that evening. Meilan worried and tried hard to persuade him to eat something; she even peeled two preserved eggs for him. Still he refused to touch the chopsticks, sitting by his desk, smoking and sighing; the wrinkles at the corners of his eyes had grown deeper and thicker. His dark face reminded her of a woodcut portrait of an old peasant kept in one of his albums.

Finally it was Shanshan who brought him around. Following her mother's instruction, she said to him, "Daddy, you're a good boy. I follow you. If you not eat, I not eat myself."

He gave the baby a smile and let out a long sigh; then he moved to the dining table and began to drink the corn-flour porridge. He noticed a cooked weevil floating in his bowl. With a pair of chopsticks he fished it out and dropped it to the floor.

Meilan wanted to tell him to stop confronting the leaders, at least for the moment. "A sparrow shouldn't match itself against a raven" — she wanted to remind him of the saying, but she remained silent, waiting for his anger to subside.

* * *

The next afternoon the workers and staff of the plant again gathered in the dining hall, listening to Secretary Liu's preliminary report on the annual achievements. Liu announced: the plant had produced 940 tons of fertilizer this production year, which surpassed the annual target by 8 percent; twenty-four families had received new housing; nine babies had been born, only one of them having violated the one-child policy; 134 workers and staff had got raises; and sixteen people had been promoted to new "fighting posts." He concluded by declaring, "This is a victorious year. The victory is due to the solidarity and united effort of the workers and cadres of our plant."

The meeting was dull. Many people dozed off or let their minds wander. But after the report, the secretary switched to another topic, Shao Bin's recent activities, which at once aroused the audience's interest.

Liu told them that Bin had been engaged in new calumnious work. He opened his leatherette briefcase and took out a sheaf of paper. "Comrades," he said, "I have ironclad evidence here. Look, this is Shao Bin's handwriting, black on white. It's a thirty-page accusation, all written in brush. My, my, handsome brushwork indeed. What labor! He must've eaten a lot of meat and eggs to have the energy for such a project. But I want to ask Comrade Young Shao a few questions here: Why don't you put more energy into your real job as a fitter? Why are you often late for work? Why are you still unable to operate a universal lathe? Why can't you fix the forklift truck, although you have tried many times? Why do you enjoy so much fabricating stories and spreading rumors against others?"

Liu slammed the paper on the table, then picked up the last page. He went on, "Here's how he slandered others. He wrote to the Commune Administration, 'I believe there is an affair between Liu Shu and Hou Nina. Please order a full inquiry.' Shao Bin, you are a crook! Nina is just about to get married. Why did you do this to her? To make her unmarriageable? Yes, I love her, but only as a comrade, just like I love my daughter. Shao Bin, you son of a turtle, you have a dirty mind. To tell you the truth, I've been thinking of taking Nina as my nominal daughter. Yes, I love her. Say whatever you want, you pathetic imbecile."

Some people chuckled, and many turned to stare at Bin. Suddenly Nina burst out wailing in the front. She jumped up, running toward the table at which Bin was sitting. Her long hair was swinging around her shoulders; a few people leaped to their feet and stopped her.

"Let me go. Let me scratch his face!" she screamed, her mouth wide open and her eyes shut.

Liu told two young women to take Nina back to her office. After they left, the hall was so quiet that people could hear Liu breathing.

"Yesterday somebody called him 'lunatic,' " the secretary continued. "He went to Director Ma's office to complain about that. I told him bluntly that I thought he was a lunatic too. Why? Comrades, look at what he did. He tried to destroy an innocent girl's life, ruin our plant's name, and in this letter he actually smears soot on lots of people's faces. I asked myself again and again, How should I handle this fellow? If I treat him as a normal man, then he will be nobody but a reactionary, a criminal. In that way I may put a comrade into the camp of the enemy class. I've known him for six years and don't think his heart is that black, so I believe he has a problem in his brain. Yes, very likely he has a mental disorder. That's why yesterday I suggested he go to the hospital for a checkup."

Some people glanced at Bin, tittering and whispering. Bin felt his face burning and knew he couldn't convince others of what had actually happened, so he remained silent.

"Before I conclude," Liu said again, "let me give Comrade Shao Bin a piece of advice. An ant can't shake a tree. If a mantis tries to stop a tractor, it will only get itself crushed. Please have second thoughts before you try again."

Liu sat down, huffing, and lifted a teacup, as director Ma got up and went to the front.

"Comrades," Ma said, "I also think Shao Bin is a lunatic. Yesterday afternoon he came to us when we were in the middle of a meeting. I told him to come another time because we were busy at the moment. All of a sudden he yelled, 'I screw your ancestors! I screw them pair by pair!' "

Some men threw their heads back, guffawing. Ma went on, "Both Hong Bao and Huang Dongfang witnessed that. Probably their ancestors were defiled by Shao Bin too." Again a few people cackled. "Comrade Shao, please leave our ancestors alone. They are dead, cold as stone, not attractive anymore. If you're not satisfied with us, let us talk and exchange views calmly. We are humans, rational beings, aren't we?"

Bin wanted to jump up and yell, "I screw your mothers and daughters!" But he controlled himself and sat there motionless; he forced himself to look out the window. In the gray sky the clouds were overlapping one another and creating different shapes like mountains, billows, reefs, fields, forests. A few dried leaves were swirling in the air and gliding into and out of his sight. He kept watching the clouds until the meeting was over.

Bin wasn't intimidated by the leaders at all. From that day on, his brush was busier than ever. Every night he kept on writing, and sometimes not until daybreak did he go to bed to sleep for two or three hours. Now that he knew Secretary Yang of the commune belonged to the same gang, he addressed the new letter of accusation to higher authorities. This time it included Yang's crime as well. He was going to send it to the administrations of the county, the prefecture, the province, and certainly a copy to the State Council in Beijing. Though it was said that under heaven all crows are black, there had to be a place where he could let out his discontent and find justice.

Who were Liu Shu and Ma Gong? Two small cadres with glib tongues, uncouth and unlettered. They were wine vessels and rice bags, their existence only burdening the earth, whereas he had read hundreds of books and was knowledgeable about strategies.

He found himself bursting with energy and able to write late into the night without fatigue.

Four

FROST FELL AT NIGHT. In Dismount Fort children began to wear felt hats or scarves when going to school in the morning. The sound of bellows could be heard everywhere in the afternoon, when many families were boiling cabbages to make sauerkraut. A few households were pickling kimchee, and there was a scent of garlic in the air.

The Shaos were upset because they couldn't pickle sauerkraut; there was no space in their room for a large crock. The corridor of the dormitory house would be blocked if such a thing was put there; also, the smell would be awful. What Meilan did instead was salt a tall jar of turnips. For storing fresh vegetables, Bin was digging a pit in the southern corner of the courtyard, near the street wall. When it began to freeze, he would place their cabbages and turnips into it and cover them up with sorghum stalks, straw sacks, and earth. By comparison, the families in Workers' Park could put their sauerkraut crocks in their outer rooms and dig vegetable pits in their backyards; some families even built brick vegetable cellars, in which beer and fruit could be stored in summer.

On Sunday, at noon, having shoveled earth out of the vegetable pit, Bin opened the southern window to let in some warm air. The loudspeaker, hung on a pole on the street, stopped playing music and began emitting static. Then a crisp female voice announced that Secretary Yang was a candidate for the position of vice chairman of the County People's Congress. This was an honor for the whole commune. Together with him, there were two other people running for the position, and the election would be held the next morning at the County Administration.

Bin was convinced that Yang was also his enemy. Obviously, Yang had passed his letter of accusation on to the plant's leaders; this was a gross violation of the Party's policy of protecting discontented masses. No doubt the three leaders were in the same clique and should be exposed together. In his new letter of accusation, Bin had written, "The three of them wear the same pair of trousers and breathe through one nostril." Now, the news of Yang's candidacy for the congress suggested to Bin a bold idea. He had to do something to prevent Yang from winning the election; the People's Congress ought to be in the hands of an honest man who would serve the people heart and soul.

On second thought, he wondered whether it was too rash to confront Secretary Yang so soon. He was merely a worker, whereas Yang was the Party boss of Dismount Fort. Would people believe what he said about Yang?

Then he remembered that a few days ago Hsiao Peng had said to him in private, "Bin, cheer up. Don't be intimidated by them. Our Maintenance supports your exposing them. Yang Chen should be reprimanded for having your letter sent to Liu Shu." Hsiao's words convinced Bin that he had grassroots support among his fellow workers. If the County Administration had the case investigated, surely there would be people willing to testify against the leaders.

So he made up his mind to deal with Yang now.

That night, he took out a big brush made of goat's hair and wrote on a large sheet of paper: "Yang Chen Always Persecutes Me!" After the ink dried, he pasted the writing on a piece of cardboard. With a pair of scissors he poked two holes at the top of the board and attached a red ribbon to it.

To him the five words looked strenuous and elegant, each as big as a brick. Finished with the work, he couldn't help appreciating his own calligraphy with squinting eyes. His wife and daughter meanwhile were sleeping in the bed near the southern window; Meilan was snoring a little, her face pale and flabby and her nostrils slightly swollen. She was twenty-eight, but already had wrinkles on her forehead and temples. A yellow towel wrapped her permed hair, to keep the curls from being crushed in her sleep. One of her legs stretched out from under the flowery quilt, displaying bluish veins beneath the skin; her foot was shapely, but the toes had ringworm nails. On her sole there was a curved cut, about an inch long, inflicted by a piece of broken glass two days before. The cut seemed to have festered, so Bin moved to the tiny medical cabinet on their oak chest and took out a vial of merbromin. With a cotton ball held at the tips of the scissors, he dabbed the red solution on her wound. The moment he was done, she kicked her foot, moaning faintly, and withdrew her leg under the quilt.

Having returned the vial to the cabinet, he resumed watching his wife and child, whose chubby face was chapped by cold wind. He heaved a sigh and felt ashamed. Logically speaking, with such handsome calligraphy, he should have been a distinguished man, at least in this town. He asked himself, Why am I still a worker if these hands are cut out for brushwork? Why on earth can't a man like me get a decent place for his family to live? Look at this room, it's a doghouse, a snail shell.

The more he thought, the worse he felt. I swear, he said to himself, I shall get a good apartment for my family sooner or later! There will be no end of bothering them if they don't give me one.

Early the next morning, after telling Meilan that he was going to the County Administration to see the designs of some propaganda posters, and that he wouldn't be late for the second shift, Bin set out for the train station. He cycled with his right hand gripping the handlebar and his left holding the placard, which was wrapped in red paper, so that people might take it to be a framed portrait or a mirror. At the train station, he locked his bicycle to a railing bar on the wooden fence; then he bought a ticket for the eight o'clock train.

Gold County was twenty miles to the west, only an hour's trip. It's a remarkable town, with historic and military importance, because it borders on the Yellow Sea and to the south there is a bay which has been used as a navy base for more than a hundred years. The Russians and the Japanese had fought over it, and in turn their fleets had occupied it.

The sun was warm, though it was a chilly day. Trees had shed their leaves, standing naked around the large plaza before Gold County Train Station. On the east, beyond rows of poplars, perched a column of Russian-made self-propelled guns, which apparently had just rolled off a train. Soldiers were sitting on them, eating breakfast and drinking water from canteens. Once in a while, dark smoke was ejected from the rear of one of those guns; the air smelled of diesel. On the north, near the entrance to a boulevard, a crowd gathered at the bus stop, men shouldering parcels and trussed fowls and piglets, and women carrying babies and baskets full of fruits, eggs, and vegetables. Bin went across to join the crowd. Then a bus came. After a good deal of pushing and shoving, he got aboard.

The election had just started when he arrived at the County Administration. The guards at the door of the conference hall didn't suspect anything when they saw Bin, who looked scholarly, walking in a meditative manner and carrying the placard with his little finger. They thought he must have been on the organizing staff or worked as an assistant to one of the candidates. The object wrapped in red paper must have been a slogan or a picture.

But once in the hall Bin turned into another man. He hastened to the stage, where Secretary Yang, a middle-aged woman, and an old man like a peasant were sitting at a long table. Behind them, in the middle of a lavender screen, hung a giant portrait of Chairman Mao; four pairs of red flags stretched upward from the Great Leader's shoulders, as though he wore gorgeous wings.

Yang had on a blue Mao suit and a black cap covering his bald crown. He was a beardless man, over fifty, and his soft skin betrayed his career as a civil official who had been well sheltered from the elements. Also on the stage stood a tall young man in wire-framed glasses, presiding over the election. With a microphone in his hand, he was explaining the rules and procedures to the voters, while the hall was still bustling with spitting, chitchatting, sniffling, and the cracking of sunflower seeds.

As he was climbing the short stairs on the right side of

the stage, Bin turned to the three hundred people sitting below. He stopped at the edge of the stage, ripped off the red paper, and raised the placard to the audience. All at once the hall was thrown into a turmoil. Many people stood up, some pushing forward to look at the words closely.

"Beautiful handwriting!" one woman said.

"He looks like a scholar, he can't be a liar."

"Wow!"

"Who could tell Yang Chen is a demon!"

"Shameless, Yang shouldn't be there," a young peasant shouted with both hands around his mouth.

"Get down, Yang Chen!"

"Yang is disqualified."

On the stage, from where they sat, the three candidates couldn't see the contents of the placard, so they got up and went over to look. At the sight of the words the woman and the old man smirked, shaking their heads and withdrawing to their seats. But Yang bellowed, "I don't know this man! It's slander, pure invention! I swear I don't know who he is." His big head jerked about as he stamped his feet; the loudspeakers in the back corners of the hall were broadcasting the thumps made by his white plastic soles.

It was true Yang didn't know Bin. Naturally, he was protesting that this was a dirty trick some people had devised against him. "I'm framed, framed for nothing!" he kept blustering, his broad mouth twitching and his nose congested. Time and again he glared at the other two candidates.

Bin interrupted him. "I know you. You don't know me? Didn't you forward my accusation letter to the leaders of the Harvest Fertilizer Plant? Didn't you overtly support them to suppress different opinions and persecute those who criticized them? I'd know your bones if you shed your skin!"

"Who are you? What the devil are you talking about?" Yang threw up his right hand.

"I am Shao Bin. Why are you so forgetful?"

Still Yang couldn't recall what wrong he had done to this man. He shouted, "I don't know you. I swear by my Communist Party membership, I don't know what hole you jumped out of!" Turning to the other candidates, he said, "Damn it, I want an investigation of this." His fleshy cheeks turned pink as he wheezed.

Two guards ran over and hauled Bin off the stage. They clutched his arms and dragged him to the exit while another man holding the placard followed behind. Meanwhile the audience was whooping, laughing, coughing, and chattering. It seems most of them didn't believe what Yang said, and many had changed their minds about his candidacy. He had been transferred to this county three years before; people did not yet know him well enough to doubt Bin's accusation.

In fact Yang had never heard of the name Shao Bin. He hadn't seen the letter of accusation either. He had merely been informed by his aide, Dong Cai, that a troublesome worker had sent him a lengthy report on the fertilizer plant's leaders. The letter had been transferred to Liu and Ma after Dong Cai had glanced through it and decided it had been written mainly out of jealousy. Of course Yang, having committed himself to other more important matters, didn't ask further about it and put it out of his mind completely. Who could expect that out of a few pages of obscure writing would jump such an extraordinary election buster? Now, Yang's candidacy was ruined, and his ambition to become the chairman of the County People's Congress in the near future was shattered.

Because of Bin's intrusion, Yang didn't get enough votes for the position. The woman, who was elected, had outrun him by thirty-four votes. In Yang's chest hatred was flaming. The moment he returned to the Commune Administration, he called the fertilizer plant. Liu answered the phone and was shaken by his superior's rage. He tried to convince Yang that Bin was merely a madman, who was fond of painting and writing indeed, but nobody would take his words seriously.

"He pretends to be a fool," Yang said huskily, "but he's smarter than both of you. The timing, the word choice, the calligraphy, and even the way he raised the placard, damn it, who can do it better?"

"Yes, Secretary Yang, he's a capable troublemaker."

"Send me a report on this man. I must know more about him."

"Yes, we'll do that immediately."

Liu was stunned, because Yang was by nature an affable man and seldom showed his temper. Without delay, he admitted his fault in not having kept closer watch on Bin and having caused such a disturbance to his superior. He promised that from now on the plant would make every effort to control this crazy man. If a similar thing happened again, he would accept any disciplinary action against himself.

Hanging up, Liu explained to Ma what had happened. For half a minute Ma was too shocked to say anything. Who would imagine a toad could grow wings and soar into the sky!

The two leaders talked about how to handle Bin this time; both of them agreed that they should remain calm and do nothing to provoke him at the moment. In their hearts, they were frightened. This mad dog Shao Bin was simply unpredictable. He was too bold and too imaginative and would do anything he took a fancy to. Unlike those puny intellectuals — the college graduates in the plant — whose faces would turn pale and sweaty and who would correct their faults the moment the leaders criticized them, this pseudo-scholar wasn't afraid of anybody. What could you do if a man feared nothing? Even the devil didn't know how to daunt a fearless man. In addition, Bin wrote and painted exceptionally well, his blasted brush always busy at night. Every now and then he had something published in a magazine or a newspaper. How, how could you stop him?

To a degree, Liu and Ma regretted that they hadn't assigned Bin an apartment. If they had done that in the beginning, they wouldn't have turned him into such a relentless enemy. But it was too late now; all they could do was adopt a quiet approach, leaving him alone for the moment, as though they hadn't heard of the election. But this didn't mean they would let him get away with it. No, they would square the account when it was the right time.

Presently they had Dongfang, the secretary of the Youth League, start a thorough investigation of Bin's family background and his activities in the past five years so as to prepare the report to Secretary Yang and also accumulate material against Bin. If they tackled him again, they would finish him off with one blow.

Five

THE WORKERS HEARD of Bin's disrupting the election, and they were impressed. They had taken him for a mere bookworm, but all of a sudden he had emerged as a man of both strategy and action. Naturally some young workers shook hands with him.

"Brother Shao, well done," one said.

"Bin," another chimed in, "you did it for us. We must show them that we workers are the masters here."

Their words moved Bin and boosted his confidence. For days he felt lighthearted and was convinced that Liu and Ma's silence meant they were shaken by what had happened at the election. Indeed, if he had undone their boss, he could ruin them easily.

Emboldened by his fellow workers' compliments, Bin decided to pursue the tottering enemy. He started pondering how to compose another cartoon about the two leaders; since the Spring Festival was around the corner, he didn't want them to have a peaceful holiday. Besides, it was the time when officials throughout China were busy raking in new perks, receiving gifts, and bribing their superiors and related powers. As a good citizen, Bin regarded it as his duty to sound a timely alarm against corruption.

After his wife and baby went to sleep, Bin ate two raw eggs directly from the shells and drank a large mug of hot malted milk. Then he began to grind the ink stick and wet a brush. Spreading a sheet of paper on the desk, he set about painting.

He drew two human figures in motion and made sure they resembled Liu and Ma. To identify them as cadres, a copy of *Handbook for Party Secretaries,* marked with the emblem of a hammer and a sickle, was inserted under Liu's arm, and a lumpy official seal was attached to Ma's broad waistband. They each had a garland of giant garlic around the neck and carried a bottle of Maotai liquor in a trouser pocket. Two packsacks full of pineapples and oranges were on their backs, and to a belt of each sack were tied a pair of fluttering roosters, upside down and with their claws bound. Around each man's knees, four large carp were twirling and gasping in a string bag, whose mouth was grasped in the man's left hand, while his right held two cartons of Great China cigarettes. In every one of their breast pockets was stuck a bundle of ten-yuan bills. The gifts were so heavy that both men dropped beads of sweat and walked with bandy legs. Yet they smiled ecstatically, the corners of their mouths reaching their ears.

Done with the drawing, Bin paused for a moment. Absently he dipped a smaller brush, made of weasel's whiskers, into the ink. What title should I give it? he wondered. "Gifts for the Spring Festival"? No, that's too flat. "On the Way Home"? No, a good title must cut to the quick, able to spur the reader and bite the enemy.

After several minutes' thinking, he wrote these words at the top of the paper: "So Hard to Celebrate a Holiday!"

The next afternoon he mailed the cartoon to *The Workers' Daily* in Beijing, a union newspaper that didn't have a large circulation but was read throughout China.

The work accomplished, Bin felt joyful. Soon his joy was replaced by ecstasy. In his mind Chairman Mao's instruction began reverberating: "The boundless joy in fighting Heaven, the boundless joy in fighting Earth, the boundless joy in fighting Man!" Those words, representing the mettle of the proletariat, warmed Bin's heart and invigorated his blood; he felt younger, as though he had eaten a lot of ginseng or deer antler. Yes, with his brush, he was ready to engage any enemy.

The secret investigation of Bin's family background and recent activities was completed. To the leaders' dismay, nothing substantial was dug up. Bin's father had been a beggar in the old China for over thirty years, all the relatives had been poor peasants, and none had ever become a target in a political movement. In this respect Bin was clean like a piece of blank paper. As for Bin himself, only a few small things were found. Two years before, when he was repairing an air blower in the plant's dining center, he had eaten four raw eggs on the sly. Later he was criticized for that, and he paid for the eggs and turned in a twelve-page self-criticism, which was still kept in his file. This case had been closed, however, and was of little use now except for proving that he wasn't an honest man. His indecency was further verified by his submitting a false voucher to Finance. The winter before, he had been sent to Ox Village to help install a water pump; he had stayed there for only two days, but he had applied for three days' reimbursement, receiving sixty fen more than he should have. Though the money was little, it showed he couldn't be trusted, especially when money was involved. His dishonesty could be attested to further by another incident: without telling anybody, Bin had once taken home a plant-owned book, *Bicycle Repairs.* Not until a fellow worker saw it in his home two months later did he bring back this piece of public property. By then, Maintenance had already purchased a new copy of the book. If a man had stolen fruit, no doubt he would steal an orchard when the opportunity turned up.

All these indecencies, however, were not weighty

enough to bring him down. In their report to Secretary Yang, in addition to describing the defects in Bin's character, the leaders had to mention the artistic works he had published and the two awards his paintings had won. It's common sense that one glamorous quality can eclipse a dozen slight blemishes. Both Liu and Ma felt that in a way they'd done Bin a favor in having the report prepared, because Secretary Yang would be more impressed by his talent and energy than interested in those trifles. If so, they might indeed create an opportunity for him. To prevent that from happening, they stressed the point that he suffered from a mental disorder and was an inefficient, unreliable worker.

The cartoon appeared in *The Workers' Daily* two weeks later. Bin was amazed that it had come out so soon; on second thought, he realized the editors would surely have wanted to publish it before the Spring Festival so as to combat the unhealthy wind in society.

Indeed the cartoon was timely enough to ruin the leaders' festive mood. After they saw it, Liu and Ma sent for Bin and planned to teach him a bloody lesson, at least making him unable to enjoy the holiday. They waited and waited, but Bin never showed up.

By no means would Bin go to their offices alone. What if they beat him black and blue? He mustn't take such a risk, having himself hurt before the festival. He wasn't that stupid and could see through them. According to

Sun Tzu's *Art of War*, among the thirty-six stratagems the most important one is to decamp in time. Yes, he had best go home as soon as possible. Damn the two idiots, they thought he didn't know about the knives up their sleeves. If they wanted to take revenge, they had better get hold of him first.

He put away his files and claw hammer, took off the work suit and oversleeves, and left for the bicycle shed. After aligning the front wheel of his National Defense with its head tube, he pedaled away without indulging in the habit of ringing the bell on the handlebar. At the entrance of the plant, he got off the bicycle and stuck a copy of the cartoon on the notice board with a piece of friction tape.

Immediately a score of workers gathered there, looking at it and talking noisily. A middle-aged woman said, "No wonder Liu Shu is so fat. Stuffed with others' meat and fish."

"No, without sweat and blood," an old man corrected her.

"Who gave them Maotai?"

"That must've cost a fortune. Who's so rich?"

"Wow! So many pineapples."

In the secretary's office the two leaders had not yet recovered from the shock delivered by the cartoon. Now all of China knew they were two corrupt officials, sucking people's blood and taking bribes. This was sheer calumny, and Shao Bin would have to pay for it. Without delay they began gathering the facts needed for proving their innocence. Neither of them had ever received garlic from anybody; in fact, Ma hated garlic, often saying he would have banned the plant if he were a god, and he wouldn't allow his wife to use it even when she cooked fish. Nor had they ever eaten a fresh pineapple, which was an exotic southern fruit. As for Maotai, it was impossible for either of them to obtain a bottle here; if you searched all of Dismount Fort, you wouldn't be able to find one. Never had Secretary Liu tasted a drop of that liquor, and he swore he had only heard of it, whereas Ma had once drunk two glasses of it in Changchun City, where he had played basketball. That was twenty years before. Nowadays there was a shortage of everything except for human beings; nobody here could possibly have the finest Chinese liquor. It was said that only at a state banquet was Maotai served, and that most of the produce of the winery was exported to Japan and South Asia. Ah, those foreigners, they always have the best Chinese stuff!

"Damn the mad dog!" Liu cursed. "If I'd ever taken a drop of Maotai, I wouldn't feel so wronged."

"Forget about Maotai," Ma said. "It tastes similar to West Phoenix, it's just a name. What should we do about him now? Wait until the festival is over?"

"No way."

They thought of sending a group of men to smash Bin's home, breaking all the pots, basins, bowls, and plates, but the Shaos lived in the department store's dormitory, which had an entrance guard on duty day and night. And it was unwise to do that, because the other residents would witness the scene. Besides, Bin's wife had a lot of relatives in the villages; those peasants wouldn't think twice about killing if they came to avenge her. How about asking the town police to detain Bin for the holiday season? This didn't seem practicable either. They heard that the young policeman Shen Li was also an amateur painter and had once taken lessons from Bin. Undoubtedly, the student would release the teacher, since by custom you ought to regard your teacher as a lifelong father, even if he had taught you just one day. Stop paying him his wages? There was no rule that allowed them to do so, unless he was a criminal.

They were still talking when Bao, the union chairman, rushed in and said loudly, "Secretary Liu and Director Ma, the plant is upside down. Lots of people are at the notice board, looking at the picture. They want to know who gave you Maotai."

"What?" Liu stood up, wringing his hands. "Screw their mothers!"

"Let's go have a look," Ma said.

They went to the front entrance, where about seventy

workers gathered, cursing and chatting. It was snowing, the gray ground becoming white. At the sight of the leaders, the crowd quieted down. Both Liu and Ma could feel the pressure of the silence, which seemed to demand that they confess everything on the spot. Liu went up the brick steps at the front of Guard's Office, and he turned around to face the workers. For some reason he felt like laughing, but he restrained himself. A snowflake landed on his nose; though tickled by it, he didn't wipe it off. Ma limped over and joined him, standing one step lower.

"Comrades," Liu shouted, then stopped to clear his throat. "Comrades, don't take this drawing seriously. Shao Bin is a lunatic and always imagines things. Director Ma can't stand the smell of garlic. You all know that. How could he take a braid of garlic as a gift?"

"Have you ever seen me eat garlic?" Ma asked.

Seeing a few people shake their heads, Liu said again, "Shao Bin painted that we each received a bag of pineapples. That's a lie. To be honest, I've never seen a fresh pineapple. I don't know how big it is. I've only eaten canned pineapple once and have no idea how people eat a fresh one. Do you peel it, or cut it, or boil it, or pickle it? Tell me how. Come on, some of you are from the South and must know how to handle a fresh pineapple."

"Cut it!" a male voice shouted from the back. Some people laughed.

"I've never eaten a pineapple either," Ma said. "Never seen one except in the movies."

"Tell me again," Liu went on, "who among you ever saw a bottle of Maotai?"

The crowd remained silent, though some eyes were still glaring at the leaders. Liu continued, "To tell you the truth, I've never seen a bottle. I don't know what it looks like, to say nothing of what it tastes like. Shao Bin's drawing is pure slander. If any of you have a bottle, show me. I'll invite you to my home and treat you to ten courses. I won't ask for more, just give me a small glass. That'll make me feel I haven't lived so long for nothing."

A woman giggled. A puff of snow was swirling around Liu's felt hat. He seized the moment and announced, "Comrades, I swear by my great-grandfather's tombstone that if I have ever seen a bottle of Maotai, if I have ever tasted a drop of Maotai, I am a cuckold!"

"Me too!" Ma shouted. Then it occurred to him that he had drunk the liquor. Good heavens, how could he take back those words in front of this mob!

Liu was shocked by Ma's declaration, and he couldn't help squinting at him.

Seeing the secretary's fat lips purplish with rage and the director's face carmine, the workers were convinced that the leaders had told the truth. They could tell that the leaders would have skinned Bin alive if they had grabbed hold of him. Lucky for him, he wasn't here. A few people at the back turned and were leaving.

Though the workers were calmed down, the cartoon spoiled the leaders' Spring Festival. Unlike other years, when they would have twice the amount of rice, meat, fish, sugar, and soybean oil a worker had, this year they took home only the same portion as everyone in the plant. It was better not to cause any discontent at the moment; but wait, they would get everything back from Shao Bin and make him serve them like a grandson.

Six

AFTER THE SPRING FESTIVAL the plant was busy gaining a head start on the production year. To keep Bin from making trouble again, the leaders assigned all of Maintenance to overhaul two boilers and replace a distiller for the Fourth Workshop, which mainly produced explosives for the People's Army. Hsiao Peng, the director of Maintenance, who used to support Bin's drawing the cartoons, now changed his mind about him, since he understood why his section was given so much work all at once. In private he told some workers about the reason; the hostility toward Bin was mounting in the workshop.

Though working two extra hours a day, Bin wouldn't complain. He got paid for overtime; besides, others in Maintenance worked the same way. At night, exhausted and heavy-eyed, he wouldn't slack in practicing brushwork. These days he was studying an ancient monograph called *The Art of Painting;* he wanted to increase the fluidity and spontaneity of his brushstrokes, particularly to master the technique of splash-ink. So far he hadn't been able to bring out the solidity and augustness of jagged rocks on paper as the book described, though he had followed the instructions closely. He thought this was probably because he worked too hard at the plant and didn't have much vital breath left in him at the end of the day. From now on, he decided, he had better dawdle more at work. So he did.

When the apricots were blooming, the plant erected a propaganda board, thirty feet by twelve, in front of the office building. In response to the current political campaign — Against the Capitalist Road — the leaders decided to increase the workers' consciousness of class struggle by strengthening their ideological education, which should start with propaganda work. Therefore a colorful board was needed. Besides, such a construction would demonstrate the progressive outlook of the cadres and workers of the plant and impress visitors and their superiors. Though the woodwork was finished, a person capable of doing the propaganda work hadn't been found yet. In the plant nobody except Bin was skilled in brushwork. The leaders, however, were determined to keep him out of this.

Bin was indeed anxious to offer his service. He hated wielding a hammer and turning a spanner in the workshop, where he couldn't avoid getting covered with dirt and grease every day. It was a job for a coolie, not for a man of his caliber. By contrast, the propaganda work would suit him better and also might turn into a longstanding job. This meant it could eventually become an official position, which might enable him to leave Maintenance for good and be promoted to cadre's rank. Understandably, he was eager to demonstrate his artistic accomplishment.

But already he had made deadly enemies of the leaders, who would by any means prevent him from displaying his expertise. How he regretted having given them so much trouble these past months. Without knowing it, he had spoiled his own opportunity, as if he had lifted a stone at an enemy but smashed his own toes.

Though unsure of his chances, Bin decided to test the water. He went to Director Ma's office, since it seemed to him that Ma wasn't as malicious as Liu. At least Ma's tongue was less glib. Bin was ready to brace himself for harsh words; as long as they gave him the job, he would endure anything. You mustn't miss a watermelon by fighting over a few sesame seeds, he kept reminding himself.

To Bin's astonishment, when he arrived, Liu was also in Ma's office. There was no way to back out, and it was impossible to test the water in Liu's presence, so Bin went ahead and recommended himself for the job.

"You think you can do the propaganda work well?" Ma asked, drumming his fingers on the table.

"Yes, I feel I'm the most qualified man in our plant."

"That's true, you're able to do the work," Liu put in. "And we indeed don't have a person here to take charge of it. You have the talent, don't you, Young Shao?"

"Yes, Secretary Liu." Bin's eyes brightened.

Liu said, "We know you're talented, but we don't want to utilize your talent. You have something to sell, but remember, we don't have to buy it from you. To tell you the truth, we have decided to hire someone from outside and let your talent rot in you. Go back and learn to do your own work well. Stop dreaming that heaven will drop a roasted quail into your mouth."

Bin was so stunned that he stood there speechless, grinding his teeth, while the leaders chortled. He wanted to spit in Liu's face, but restrained himself. Without a word he turned to the door.

"An ass eats in every trough," said Liu.

Bin turned back. "You mustn't insult me. You must respect my human dignity and —"

"Stop that!" Liu stood up, pointing at Bin's nose. "I know that a petty intellectual like you always wants to get laid, but even though you pull down your pants and raise your butt, I won't be aroused. No, we can't use you, not interested, period!"

Ma blew his nose on a piece of letter paper, chuckling some more. Bin couldn't stand this any longer. "I'll make asses of you two!" he yelled, flourishing his right arm as though wielding a brush.

* * *

For days, whenever possible, Bin would pass the office building to see who had been hired for the propaganda work; but he found nobody at the board, whose naked wood remained smooth and white, waiting for the touch of an artistic hand. Not until a week later did he find a short man there putting primer on the board. The man was squatting on his haunches, his knees wide open, and from time to time his broad buttocks almost touched the ground. He was wielding a large brush; a pail of black paint stood nearby. Though Bin couldn't see his face, the pudgy body looked familiar to him, especially the thick neck and round shoulders. After watching for a few minutes from a distance, Bin went over to see who he was.

His footsteps drew the attention of the man, who turned around, revealing his broad eyes and dark brows. Bin was surprised to find it was Yen Fu, an acquaintance of his. Yen was an art cadre in Gold County.

"How are you, Master Shao?" Yen said, and stood up with a puzzled look on his face. He stretched out his hand.

"I'm all right, still alive."

They shook hands. Yen's big mouth opened a little but didn't succeed in making a smile; he seemed embarrassed.

After a few words with Yen, wishing him a good time here, Bin left, feeling further humiliated, because Yen wasn't a good painter. Three years ago they had met in Shenyang City, when Bin had won third prize for a landscape painting exhibited in the Provincial Gallery. Yen sought him out, and together they shared a Mongolian firepot at a restaurant; while eating, Yen expressed his admiration for Bin's work. That was why just now Yen had called him Master Shao.

Despite working as the art editor for a small newspaper called *Environment,* Yen was indeed artistically inferior to Bin in most ways. He had never expected to encounter the "master" here, assuming Bin had left the plant long ago. How could a small pond like this contain such a big fish? He had vaguely heard that Bin was teaching the fine arts somewhere.

After meeting Bin, Yen felt he had been taken in by the plant's leaders and had done a stupid thing, displaying his skills before a superior hand. To make up for this blunder, the next evening he bought a bottle of sorghum liquor and two yuan's worth of pig-blood sausages and paid a visit to Bin. He was pleased that Bin received him as a friend and even insisted they have a drink together.

Since the Shaos had already had dinner, Meilan scrambled four duck eggs, made a salad of jellyfish and cabbage, and sliced the sausages Yen had brought along. After that, she wiped the chopping board clean, washed her hands, and resumed crocheting a pillowcase. She sat cross-legged on the bed while Shanshan played in her lap.

The dining table, oval and one foot tall, was set on the

earth floor. Bin placed on it the dishes, two cups, and a porcelain liquor pot.

Meanwhile Yen was sitting at the writing desk, sipping tea. He noticed Bin's crablike ink slab and asked, "What stone is this?"

"Bring it here," Bin said. "I'll explain it while we're eating."

Yen sat down and put the stone on the dining table. "Don't treat me like a guest, Master Shao."

"Call me Bin or Old Shao, all right?"

"All right, Bin," Yen said out loud.

They both laughed, so did Meilan. "For our friendship," they said almost with one voice, raising the cups.

While chewing a chunk of sausage, Bin began to talk about the ink slab. "This is a Gold Star stone, quarried from Fei County, Shandong Province, the only place that produces this kind of stone." He moved the slab closer to Yen. "See these speckles? They are the stars. The ancients said, 'It's hard to wear away an iron ink slab.' They referred to this kind of dark slab. In fact, Gold Star stones aren't that hard. It's an exaggeration. These starlets are bits of mica. At night, when you gaze at these speckles at the bottom of the inkwell, you feel like you are watching the Dippers. Under the stars the night is damp and deep, and villages, towns, cities all are asleep, while you're busy working alone. If you gaze long and intently enough, you'll forget it's an ink slab, and you'll have the sight of a vast landscape. In a word, it's a very poetic stone, very poetic."

Yen was impressed by Bin's knowledge about ink slabs. He mentioned that there was an antique store in Gold County, which they should visit together someday.

Suddenly the baby gave a forceful wail. "What happened?" Bin asked his wife.

"She wet my skirt," Meilan said, and turned to Shanshan. "How many times have I told you to tell me before you pee? Huh, brat?"

The baby cried some more and dropped her rubber doll on the floor. Meilan stood up, the front of her beige skirt carrying a wet patch as large as a Ping-Pong paddle.

"Come on," Bin said to his wife, "take care of her, will you? Brother Yen is here."

Meilan walked over to the wardrobe and took out a pair of pants for the child and a dress for herself. Then she picked up Shanshan; with the baby on her right hipbone, she walked out.

Yen thought the Shaos must have had another room in the house where she could change, so he asked Bin, "You have another room?"

"No, she went to the salesgirls' bedroom, across the hall."

They went on to talk about the painters and calligraphers they knew. It happened that every one of them was doing better than Bin; even Yen had gained two promotions in rank in the past three years, whereas Bin hadn't even got a raise in the meantime. This aroused his anger again.

He said, "The fertilizer plant is a loony bin. I envy you, Brother Yen."

"You should've been an art cadre long ago, Bin. This isn't a place for you."

What can I do?"

"It's a waste of talent. Logically speaking, I should do your work, and we should switch places. A crazy world, isn't it?"

Meilan returned in a saffron dress. Yen found her almost a different woman now, delicate and rather pretty, especially when seen from behind. The dress had shrunk her and brought out her trim waist, but the baby remained the same, in the same kind of open-butted pants.

Yen was curious to learn why the plant's leaders didn't let Bin do the propaganda work. Bin sighed and told him the whole story, from the first cartoon to his recent confrontation with them. After his account of the events, he said gloomily, "Ever since the ancient times, too big a piece of wood can't be used to make furniture. It's my fate."

"He's too stubborn," Meilan said to the guest. "I begged him to give in a bit just for once, but he wouldn't."

Yen said, "It's no use fighting with them all the time. I understand how you feel, Bin, but a wise man doesn't fight when the odds are against him."

"I don't want to fight. They would never leave me alone. They engage me themselves; so damned bloodthirsty."

"How about this: tomorrow I'll talk with them, put in a good word for you, and ask them to stop mistreating you. I don't know whether it will help. It seems worth trying. What do you think?"

"Please do it," Meilan broke in. "We can't continue to live like this. They should give him the bonus and an apartment."

Bin smiled acquiescently.

The next day at noon, the two friends met at the plant's dining center. Yen informed Bin that the leaders would like to talk to him, and that he should go to Liu's office at three in the afternoon. "They seemed to listen to me," Yen said. "I told them you are the ideal man for the propaganda work, and you can teach me. Boy, they were impressed." He raised his left eyebrow; Bin thanked him.

They wouldn't sit together to eat lunch, fearing the leaders would suspect any abnormal relationship between them. Bin took his lunch — two baked wheaten cakes and a plate of fried eggplant — to the coal pile in the yard and joined a group of fellow workers there, while Yen ate inside the dining hall.

Bin was somehow possessed by a kind of mysterious joy after the noon break. A man of merit never lacks friends, he thought. Yen is a good brother of mine, a true man with a kind heart. That's why his painting and calligraphy have developed so much; he's beginning to have his own style. Bin had in mind the golden characters Yen had inscribed on the propaganda board: "We Resolutely Oppose Capitalist Deviations!"

For some reason two lines of Tang farewell poetry went on ringing in his ears:

> Do not worry about having no friend on the road;
> Under heaven who has not heard of your name?

In the outhouse near the garage, he even chanted out the lines three times while urinating into a long cement trough constructed as a urinal. A woman tittered beyond the brick wall, from the female side of the outhouse. The tittering sobered him up, since he didn't want the name of a latrine poet.

At two-fifty he set out for the secretary's office, after informing Hsiao that the leaders wanted to meet with him. When he arrived at the office, both Liu and Ma were in there, smoking and laughing, talking with Nina. The ceiling fan was revolving briskly; beneath it a few houseflies were droning. On the desk a bunch of daylilies stood in a beer bottle; the room smelled grassy. At the sight of Bin, they stopped laughing and regained their normal appearance. Nina got up and walked to the door with her ponytail whisking slightly on her back. Passing Bin, she gave him a sullen look.

"Sit down, young Shao," Liu said, patting a chair.

"Have some tea," Ma said amiably, and pointed to a green porcelain cup with a lid on it.

Bin sat down and thanked them. He lifted the cup, took off the lid, blew away the floating tea leaves, and took a sip. His mouth couldn't help smiling, revealing his uneven teeth.

"Comrade Shao Bin," Liu said, "we're going to inform you of something."

Bin nodded expectantly.

"Your friend Yen Fu is a good talker," Liu resumed. "He has convinced us that you are a budding genius. You know our plant is not a large unit. Only three hundred people here, it's too small a pond for a large turtle like you, so we hope you'll transfer to another place that can offer you a suitable job. We won't keep you here and let you miss the opportunity to develop your talent. You see, we are always concerned with our young people's growth."

"Yes, when you find a new place that's willing to accept you, we'll let you go," Ma added with a sneer.

Bin remained wordless, never having thought they would get rid of him like this. So they have me here only to give me a hard time and make me miserable, he reasoned. Damn you, idiots. You two did your calculation on a wrong abacus. I'm not leftovers that nobody will touch.

As the leaders were smirking and observing his confused face, Bin stood up and said stridently, "All right, I shall try."

"You know," Liu said, "your problem is that you always believe you know exactly how high the sky is and how deep the sea is. You're a smart jackass."

"That's true," Ma put in. "You overestimate yourself all the time."

Without responding, Bin turned to the door and walked out with his back and neck straight. However, the moment he was out of the office, he felt giddy, overwhelmed by hatred and confusion. He had to hold the iron handrail to descend the stairs.

Yen visited Bin in the evening. When Bin told him what had happened in the office, Yen was outraged. The leaders' breach of promise verified Bin's account of their evil nature and deeds. They would lie to your face. This time they had tricked not only Bin but also Yen himself, to whom Liu and Ma had given their word that they would improve Bin's standing in the plant and utilize his learning and talent. Now, they were trying to drive him out. What a bunch of hoodlums. How could any decent human being work and live under their leadership? No wonder Bin had a hellish time here.

After cursing the leaders together for half an hour, they began talking about the matter of a job transfer. What had seemed disastrous at first didn't look so bad after careful consideration. It was too exhausting to stay in this mad water and fight against those unscrupulous men, with too much of Bin's energy and time being dissipated. As an artist, he needed peace of mind for artistic creation and development, and needed concentration, especially in his formative years. Everybody knows tranquillity is the soil in which talent grows. But in a place like this, with one trick after another, nobody could live artistically; and just one unhappy incident would ruin a few days, during which any real work was impossible. Bin ought to find a more nurturing place.

Yen was almost certain some work units would take a man of Bin's ability. He promised that he would help him look for a job in the county town.

When Yen was leaving, it was already past eleven; both Shanshan and Meilan had fallen asleep in the bed. Bin walked Yen all the way to East Wind Inn opposite the train station. The air was full of the fragrance of pagodatree blossoms, which were shimmering like snow in the moonshine. Somehow even the pulverizer, which always rumbled in the distance at the fertilizer plant, became silent tonight. The railroad track, lit by a string of lights, curved gradually and disappeared into the dark mountain. The town was asleep and peaceful.

Yen inhaled the intense air and said, "What a beautiful night! Nature is so good."

"Only man is not," added Bin.

They both laughed. Their laughter was free and gusty in the quiet night.

Bin said, "God, I haven't laughed like this for a long time."

At the entrance to the inn, an old drunk, a crippled peasant, stopped them and begged for money. Yen gave him a five-fen coin, waving him away. The two friends then said good-bye.

From the next night on, Bin began to write letters to editors and art cadres who he thought might be interested in hiring him. To be sure, he used a good brush, the new one with sturdy marten's hair, and made every word look handsome and masculine, every line straight and well measured, and every page evenly distributed with lovely characters. He informed the recipients that he had an urban residence card, which allowed him to live in any city, and that he didn't expect to have housing and a high salary. His family could stay in Dismount Fort for the time being, and once he settled in the new place, he would try to find housing for them by himself.

He understood he had to make his way step by step. It would be foolish to appear too expensive in the beginning.

Seven

BECAUSE OF HIS BAD MOOD, Bin couldn't paint or practice calligraphy for two weeks. His brushes seemed to have lost their vigor, drooping in the pot cut from a tin can. The need to find a new work unit grew more and more urgent, and the anxiety became insupportable. Meilan often felt her husband was as tense as a clock wound up every hour.

Whenever Bin ran into Liu or Ma, they would ask him whether he had found a place yet; with false smiles they would advise him to be flexible, not to demand too much. At a meeting they even announced to the plant that Bin was going to leave of his own choice, which they fully supported.

One day in early May, Bin received a letter from Gold County's Cultural Center, which notified him that they would like to "borrow" him from the plant for a year, and they might keep him if everything worked out properly.

He would be given an office and a small fund for stationery. The letter also said the center had already written to the Harvest Fertilizer Plant for his file.

Having read the letter three times, Bin felt his blood circulating again. He had been afraid that the frustration and depression might turn him into a true misanthrope, really worthy of the nickname Man Hater. Now, he realized there were still decent human beings on the earth, and by nature not all men were bad.

The next afternoon he came across Secretary Liu in the changing room of the bathhouse. Liu, standing on a long bench, was taking off his undershirt; his columnar thighs were clothed in red shorts. Bin, done with bathing, was walking to the door, buttoning his shirt with one hand and holding a basin in the other. Seeing nobody near Liu, he moved close and asked, "Secretary, have you received a letter from the county's Cultural Center?"

"Oh yes." Liu put his hands behind the elastic waist of his silk shorts, about to take them off; but he changed his mind, pulled out his hands, and sat down on the bench.

"So you'll let me leave?" Bin asked.

"Director Ma and I have considered that. Unfortunately, no. It can't be so easy. We don't want to 'lend' you to anyone. We just wrote them back and insisted that if they really want you, they must take you for good and never send you back. Our plant has a fixed quota of employees. You can't keep your position here while working for others. We want you to leave for good, so we can use the quota to hire someone else. It's unfair that you occupy the latrine if you don't crap."

"Damn you!" Bin cursed, tears gathering in his eyes. "You promised to let me go! Why did you change your mind? Why?" He shook the white basin, in which his soapbox and slippers clacked.

Liu cringed a little. Then seeing two men at the other end of the room, he regained his composure. He said, "It's true we promised that, but we didn't say you could leave this way, did we?" He chuckled, resting his left foot on the bench and fondling his big toe.

Bin realized he had been tricked again. The two leaders meant to make him suffer and enjoyed seeing him miserable. "There'll be no end between us!" Bin said through his teeth, and stomped out of the bathhouse.

The leaders had never expected an important place like Gold County's Cultural Center would be interested in Bin. To some extent, they were scared by the breakthrough in his job search. The official letter stated clearly that Bin might become an art cadre in the future if their quota allowed. How could Liu and Ma let him occupy such an important position? That would be like allowing a caged tiger to return to its native mountain or a poisonous snake to grow wings, turning into a wild dragon. Once they lost control over him, he would write and paint in any way he pleased and would certainly take revenge on them. Understandably, Liu and Ma changed their minds and were determined to keep Bin in their hands.

However, the process of job transfer had started and couldn't be stopped overnight. Within two weeks, a newspaper owned by the Dalian Railroad Company and a magazine of folk arts each sent people to the plant to read Bin's file and make arrangements for transferring him to their editorial offices. Both Liu and Ma were impressed by the arrivals of these visitors, never having thought Bin was so resourceful. The two propaganda units were each willing to offer him an excellent job, of which neither Liu nor Ma would ever dream for his own children. It was evident that once he became an art cadre, Bin would make them stink beyond the radius of a hundred miles; he was so narrow-minded that he might try to ruin their children as well; therefore, at any cost, they must not let him go. Liu told the visitors, "We are glad that you'd like to take Comrade Shao Bin. We won't keep him; but you must promise us one thing."

"What?"

"You will never send him back."

"Why?"

"Mental," Ma said, his forefinger pointing at his temple with the thumb cocked up. One of his eyes was shut as though he were in pain.

That was enough to scare anyone away. Having heard

those words, one pair of the visitors didn't bother to read Bin's file and left the plant within ten minutes.

Bin was informed by the newspaper and the magazine that the plant's leaders thought him inadequate for the jobs. Outraged as he was, he couldn't figure out why the leaders had changed their minds.

When he asked them for an explanation a week later, Ma yawned and told him plainly, "We do want to help you find a decent 'home,' but you're such an important man that we have to get Secretary Yang's permission to let you go."

"Yes," Liu chimed in. "Secretary Yang wants to keep you here for some special use in the future. He told us to take good care of you."

They laughed, seeing that he believed them. Ma sneezed and spat on the floor, though a yellow spittoon sat in a corner of his office.

As if struck by a calamity, Bin couldn't control his tears anymore. He rushed out of the office, his heart pounding. Once he was outside, tears flooded his cheeks; he put his palm over his mouth to prevent himself from wailing out. Never had he expected Secretary Yang would interfere with the job transfer.

If Yang was so determined to keep him in his clutches, it meant Bin would be stuck in this madhouse for good. How he regretted having disrupted the election six months before! Again, without a second thought he had laid a trap for himself.

That evening he told his wife about Yang's interference; Meilan was so disappointed that she said it served him right and he had asked for it. Everyone understood the importance of peaceful coexistence, even a first grader knew that, but Bin, a man of almost thirty-two, had purposely provoked a clash with the commune's Party secretary. Nothing good would come of this. He had set himself on fire.

Bin didn't talk back, realizing he had indeed acted too rashly. What a painful lesson. He rapped his chest with his fists now and then.

The Office of Workers' Education had been encouraging young employees to take the college entrance exams in June. The previous year nobody in the plant had entered for them, whereas many factories and companies in the county had one or two persons that had passed the exams and got enrolled in a college or a professional school. This was not good for the image of the plant, and therefore Secretary Liu announced at a meeting that the leaders supported whoever would compete in the exams. "We don't want others to think we are an illiterate tribe," Liu told the staff and workers. "If any of you would like to try, we'll give you two weeks to prepare yourself. Our plant will pay you for doing that."

Nobody dared try except Bin. When he entered his

name for the exams, both the leaders laughed and thought he'd gone berserk again. First, he was overage; no school was accepting a freshman older than twenty-eight. Second, he had only five years' elementary education; although he was capable of wielding a brush and throwing out a few lines of ancient poetry once in a while, by no means could he handle the systematic exams in mathematics, chemistry, physics, political science, ancient Chinese and literature, and a foreign language — English or Japanese or Russian. So they let him put in his name, provided he wouldn't withdraw under any circumstances. Bin promised he would not; at all costs he had to leave the plant. The leaders were pleased that he had begun weaving a net for himself again, and they expected to make him a laughingstock.

Eight

IN DISMOUNT FORT streets were swept and walls whitewashed. Slogans were posted on tree trunks and electrical poles; paper flowers, red flags, and colorful bunting decorated porches and gates; all the windows facing the streets were washed and wiped clean. The town had just launched a crackdown on flies, mosquitoes, mice, and bedbugs. The air was heavy with the smell of dichlorvos.

A conference on the use of methane in country households was going to be held here, and several important officials from the provincial capital would be present. Dismount Fort had been chosen to host the conference because Willow Village in the commune had finished constructing methane pits for all its households. For cooking and lighting, the villagers began to use the gas produced from rotten vegetables, grass, and manure. The village was the first one methanized in the province, and it became a model. In Dismount Fort, many brick walls carried slogans in whitewash, such as UTILIZE METHANE, TURN WASTE INTO TREASURE; SAVE ENERGY RESOURCES TO BUILD OUR MOTHERLAND; METHANIZATION IS A GREAT CAUSE; ANSWER THE PARTY'S CALL, BEAUTIFY OUR HOMES."

At a preparatory meeting, both Secretary Yang and Chairman Ding Liang of the commune emphasized that hosting the conference was the principal task at the moment and that everybody ought to participate in the preparations. These days the amplifier in the corridor of the dormitory house where the Shaos lived kept announcing Willow Village's achievement.

Bin had seen most of the slogans, but he had to remain uninvolved, because he was going to take the college entrance exams in a few days. He noticed that all the big characters on the walls were badly written. They looked shaky, hardly able to stand on their own; only because they were lined up together did the words appear rather neat, keeping each other from falling down. What is more, he didn't find a single painting or poster in town. What a shame, he said to himself; a commune of over thirty thousand people can't find a man capable of doing a propaganda poster. For sure the visitors will think there's no talent here.

If he had not been busy cramming for the exams, Bin would have gone to the Commune Administration and volunteered to paint a few pieces — to impress that bureaucrat Secretary Yang. But he had to work on math and political economics now. Fortunately, he had just been informed that no foreign language was required in his case, because he had applied for the fine arts; neither would he have to take physics or chemistry. He was to write only three exams: math, Chinese language and literature, and politics. Ten days before, he had mailed a bunch of photographs of his paintings and calligraphy and a list of his publications to three colleges, hoping his work would impress some professors, so that they might treat him as an outstanding applicant. Now he had to concentrate on math. Day and night he was lost in a maze of algebraic equations, logarithms, and trigonometric functions, of which he had never heard before and which made his head throb. Yet he persevered.

There was no time to review literature, classical Chinese, the history of the Chinese Communist Party, or dialectical materialism. He would have to depend on his general knowledge and common sense to tackle the questions in those areas. If only he could have had a year or two to study them. The more he pored over the math books, the more disappointed he became; from time to time he had to restrain a wild impulse to tear the textbooks to pieces.

One morning in late June, Bin took the five o'clock train to Gold County, with three fountain pens stuck in his breast pockets and six sodas and twenty hard-boiled eggs in his army satchel. He was to take the exams at a middle school and stay there overnight. On the train he ran into a group of students who were from the Bearing Factory's middle school in Apple Town and were going to take the entrance exams too. Bin talked with two of the boys and found that their exam location was the same as his. They assured him that he could follow them to the school; this was a relief for Bin, because he didn't know how to get there. They arrived at the school at eight, just in time.

First came math, which was disastrous. Most of the problems were simply incomprehensible to Bin, and he had to skip them. Section One, the algebraic calculation, didn't seem very difficult at first glance, but he was stuck on a complex quadratic equation and simply couldn't recall the formula that he had just reviewed on the train two hours ago. As a result, he had to leave more than half of this section untouched; then he moved ahead to attack the verbal problems. The first one alone, about the efficiency ratio of a bulldozer and shovels and picks, which initially looked very simple, took him almost an hour. After that, his eyes began aching, yet he compelled himself to do as much as he could. Time and again he looked through the four large sheets — most of the problems were well beyond his knowledge. He was sweating all over and kept murmuring to himself, I shouldn't be here.

He looked around. The others were all busy writing.

The room was so quiet that he heard their pens rustling. He gazed at the faces on the right and then on the left; the boys and girls were so young; by contrast, he was almost old enough to be their father. It was foolish for him to compete with these fully educated teenagers, to seek humiliation. He felt heartbroken, but he reined in his wandering mind and forced himself to work on another verbal problem.

The bell rang. Every page of his exam paper remained almost blank, and he felt so embarrassed that he turned the sheets over when handing them back to the teacher. Walking out of the schoolhouse with others who were chattering, comparing notes, and complaining, Bin felt uncertain about even the few problems he had solved. Perhaps he had not given any correct answer. He tried to forget the math and pull himself together for the next exam, though from time to time a miserable feeling overwhelmed him.

Despite his dark mood, he ate six eggs at noon. He sat under a large elm at the side of a playground, leafing through his notes and reviewing the answers to some general political questions. The pagoda trees around him had shed their blossoms, but there was still a touch of the sweetish scent in the air. In the shade of the trees some parents were busy serving lunch and fanning their teenage children, who were resting for the next exam. The sight of parental love made Bin feel lonely. Nobody had ever treated him with such care; his father had often kicked him and whipped his backside with wickers. "A man has to stand alone," he mumbled.

Politics came next. At the first part — the multiple-choice section, he was baffled after looking through the questions. It took him almost five minutes to decide on the first choice, on which he was supposed to use no more than one minute. Then he made a prompt decision and ticked all the B's as the answers to the remaining eleven questions. He wanted to save time for the major part, the four short essays, in which he could bring his pen into full play. He spent over two hours on them and wrote long and well, especially the one on the criterion of truth. But he hadn't completed the section on the History of the Chinese Communist Party before the bell tinkled in the hallway. If only he could have had ten more minutes. Yet on the whole, the political exam was much less difficult to him.

Still, as he turned in the sheets and left the room, his legs felt heavy, as though a pair of sandbags had been attached to the calves. He couldn't help repeating to himself, I'm old, and shouldn't compete with these smart kids. Again he regretted having attempted the exams. Without any hesitation he had put his face on show. There could be no chance for him to pass, and no school would take a man his age. In fact, only about 1 or 2 percent of these youths would be admitted by a college; even if he had scored good marks, his chance would have remained close to zero.

Bin shared a dormitory room at the school with three boys who couldn't return home for the night. Though he had forgotten to bring along a blanket, it wasn't too bad; the lodging was free, and the boys were quiet, all busy cramming for the next day.

Normally, the Chinese language and literature should have been easy for him, but he didn't do well on the last exam. The translation of ancient Chinese into the modern language was fine; the identification of the authors of some lines of classical poetry went well too; there was no problem in the sentence making and the phrase forming either. The trouble occurred in the composition, which made up 60 percent of the mark.

The assigned topic was "Whenever I sing 'The East Is Red and the Sun Is Rising.'" As Bin was working at it, somehow his talent for drama took over. His pen wandered into a story, in which many of his fellow workers sang the song together every morning as a way to get their day started. Once on this dramatic course, his pen galloped along with abandon. To set up a scene, the narrator even mentioned snowflakes flying like goose feathers and pine branches tapping on the windowpanes when the workers indoors were singing the song that warmed their hearts and blood.

Not until the last moment did it dawn on Bin that he was supposed to write an essay, not a story, to express his profound love for Chairman Mao, who, though he had passed away, was shedding happy rays on the Chinese nation like the sun in the sky. Oh, it was too late to restart it; the bell burst out jingling. He tried to write a few more sentences to give the story a curt, essayistic ending, but the woman teacher grabbed the sheets from him, the others having already turned theirs in.

Bin returned home with a sullen face and a boil on his gum. But at the sight of him, Meilan beamed with two dimples, saying, "Good news." She handed him a white envelope.

He started to read the letter. It was from Professor Gong Zheng of the Department of Fine Arts at the Provincial Teachers University. The professor informed Bin that his colleagues and he were so impressed by the photographs of his work and his publications that they would accept him as a special student, since he was too old to be a freshman.

Bin couldn't help smiling; his tears fell on the thin paper. "They're going to accept me. He-he-he, they accept me!" he cried out, and held his wife up by the waist, swinging her around. One of her flying heels scraped Shanshan's shoulder and knocked her down.

The baby burst out crying, not only because of the fall but also because she saw her father's tears and thought her parents were fighting. Bin held Shanshan up and kissed her on the cheek. "Good girl, don't be scared. We'll go to Shenyang City together. Dad is so happy. You know, there're giant pandas in the zoo there. Don't you want to see a giant panda? Tell Daddy, yes or no?"

"Uh-huh." The baby was rubbing her eyes with the back of her soiled hand.

Meilan took out a bowl of fried mackerel she had prepared for the celebration, and Bin opened a bottle of date wine whose sweet flavor his wife liked best. The couple clinked glasses again and again while eating the fish; Shanshan had a small cup too, but she didn't like the fish and ate sliced melon instead. They reminisced about the prophecy by Blind Bea, the secret fortune-teller in town, who had revealed to them three years ago that at the age of thirty-two things would change in Bin's favor. Apparently the prophecy was coming true. Meilan declared she'd always believed in Bin's ability to earn more than a common worker, and that was why she had married him. Her words almost moved him to tears again.

She turned on the radio for some music. The tune of "Happy Heaven and Blissful Earth" floated in the room, but a moment later Secretary Yang's caressing voice cut short the music and began speaking about the significance of the methane conference. Yang insisted that there should be a festive atmosphere in town tomorrow and that everybody must show civil virtues to the visitors. His voice dampened the happy air at the dining table. Bin turned gloomy and stopped talking, his face long and his nostrils quivering. What should I do if Yang interferes again? he thought. Surely Yang won't let me go to college; he had made up his mind to smother me in this place.

Meilan read Bin's thoughts and asked, "Are you afraid Yang will stop you again?"

Bin nodded and sighed.

This time they had to figure out a way to prevent Yang from stepping in. But the seed of animosity had been sown deep, and it was impossible to make it up with Yang in a short time.

Besides, Bin was merely a worker, so there was no way for him to approach the town's Party boss. The truth was that once he bent his knees, he would become nothing in Yang's eyes, and any gesture of reconciliation from his side would make the enemy swell up with arrogance, more eager to crush him.

After an hour's discussion, the couple decided to take preemptive measures. They believed that only after Bin proved himself too powerful for Yang to suppress would the secretary set him free. Begging for mercy would not help.

That night Bin worked out a letter of complaint addressed to the provincial leaders. He used the smallest brush and wrote in the Regular Script, which was meant to demonstrate his knowledge of the ancient formality in legal matters. He supposed that if the readers of the letter were impressed by the calligraphy, they would inevitably be convinced that the writer was a virtuous scholar. The letter listed Yang's wicked deeds against Shao Bin, a knowledgeable, revolutionary worker who had been persecuted again and again, simply because he was artistic and outspoken. It consisted of only four pages, but it took him three hours to finish.

Nine

AFTER BREAKFAST, Bin put the letter of complaint into his inner breast pocket and went to the theater in the marketplace, where the conference was to be held. Usually by this hour the country fair in the marketplace would be bustling with people, animals, poultry, vegetables, fruits, the explosions of corn poppers, the clanking of hammers, the croaking of bellows, the jangling of iron-rimmed cart wheels. But today it was quiet. All the vendors and craftsmen had been ordered to go to the plaza in front of the train station. At the entrance to the marketplace, a large notice was posted on a granite wall, directing customers to the plaza for the fair.

Seeing a few militiamen from a distance, Bin put on his shell-rimmed glasses, which at once made him resemble an official participant in the conference. He walked deliberately with his feet splayed, once in a while taking a puff on a cigarette, as though pondering something.

Nobody stopped him all the way to the theater. He went through the front door, made of jujube wood. Inside, a large crowd was gathering. Bin planned to wait among the people; not until all the attendants took their seats and the leaders were introduced would he ascend the stage. He would go directly to the highest-ranking official from the Provincial Administration and present to him the letter of complaint with both hands; then he would shout to the audience: "Yang Chen suppresses the revolutionary masses in this commune! Down with the bureaucrat Yang Chen! Give us an upright Party secretary!" He wanted to make it as dramatic as possible, so dramatic that Yang wouldn't be able to explain it away in front of hundreds of people and dozens of his superiors.

Bin had not yet decided where to sit when Secretary Liu came up to him. "What are you doing here, Shao Bin?" he asked sharply.

"Just looking around."

"This isn't a place for window-shopping. Go back to the plant and work."

Director Ma hurried over too. He had seen Bin a moment before but mistaken him for an official because of Bin's glasses. Liu's voice had helped him identify his worker.

Ignoring Liu, Bin moved aside to take a seat.

"Come, let's get out of here," Liu hissed, and grasped him by the upper arm.

Ma went forward and grabbed his other arm, cursing, "Damn you, you can't live without making trouble."

Bin was struggling to free himself, shouting, "Help! Help! They're kidnapping me! Save my life!"

People stood up, and some were coming over to watch. "Who kidnapped you?" Ma cried, pulling Bin closer. He was so outraged he hit him in the crotch with his knee.

"Oh!" Bin dropped to the floor, gasping and moaning. He was lying on his back with both hands covering his crotch, his legs stretching out in the shape of a flock of flying geese.

For a moment, neither of the leaders knew what to do with this man who was pretending to be paralyzed. Then the union chairman Bao and a few young men arrived and tried to persuade Bin to get up. But Bin refused to budge and kept his eyes shut.

Liu stepped closer and said through his teeth, "I knew you'd show up today, you are so addicted to upsetting meetings. Now, if you don't get up I'll finish you off right here. Son of a rabbit, get up!"

Still Bin didn't move. Ma bent down and pinched his cheek, but Bin only responded with a groan. To everyone's surprise, Liu raised his foot to straddle Bin's head and dropped his large bottom on Bin's face. "All right," he said, "I'm smothering you to death on the spot."

Under Liu's weight, the rims of Bin's glasses snapped, and a lens fell out on the cement floor. Ma stepped forward and ground it to bits with his leather heel. Bin couldn't breathe and stopped making noise, feeling his limbs grow numb as though they were no longer his own. Liu's bottom, smelling of onion, was so heavy that Bin realized he would faint in a few seconds if he didn't take action. So he wiggled his head a little and took a big bite.

"Ah!" Liu jumped up, apparently crippled. With his right hand covering his hip, he was hobbling away and screaming, "Oh, my butt. He bit my butt!" His forefinger pointed back at Bin while the palm was rubbing his hip.

Ma kicked Bin in the thigh and motioned to his men. "Get him out of here."

They lifted Bin's upper body and dragged him to the entrance, while Bin kept shouting, "They broke my balls and glasses!"

"It's a madman," someone said to the people who couldn't get through the crowd to look.

"A lunatic bit his leader," another added.

Sitting on a boulder outside the theater, Bin tried to collect his thoughts. Spasms were seizing his lower abdomen, and he believed his testicles were swollen with dark blood. They were so painful that he couldn't stand up and walk home. Fortunately, Hsiao Peng happened to be at the theater and offered to take him home by bicycle.

They arrived at the dormitory house fifteen minutes

later. Meilan was not in. Bin felt sorry that he couldn't make tea for Hsiao, but he said he wasn't thirsty. As Hsiao was about to leave, Bin tentatively asked him whether he would mind giving witness to the beating. Hsiao said plainly, "Forget it, Young Shao. Why do you enjoy fighting so much? Nothing good will come of it if you go on like this, you know? Don't think of fighting anymore, all right? Think about your work and your family."

"What do you mean by my 'work'?" Bin's voice turned angry. "You mean I haven't worked well."

"Yes, you only know how to mess things up. To be honest, I wish you weren't in our Maintenance. Who can keep watch on you all the time?"

"Did they ask you to do that? To be responsible for what I do?"

"Damn, you understand everything but never try to change. You must change yourself."

Bin remained silent as Hsiao raised the door curtain, which was made of strings of glass beads, and walked out. "Coward," he cursed Hsiao under his breath.

How embarrassing to be hurt like this. Bin felt too ashamed to go to the Commune Clinic, where he would have to show the bruise to a doctor or a nurse. All he could do was cover the purple area with a flat bottle of cold water. Meilan cried and wanted to go to the leaders and curse them and their ancestors, but he dissuaded her. It was no use quarreling with those savages who knew only one language: brute force.

Unlike Bin, Liu didn't mind showing the bite on his rear to others. Before the conference was adjourned for lunch and a nap, he left for the photo shop, which was on Main Street, near the entrance to the marketplace. Since the fair had been moved, few customers were in the shop. When Liu arrived, the photographer Jia Cheng was reading *Evergreen News,* the town's newspaper, and smoking a pipe in the dim waiting room.

"Old Jia," Liu said, "can you take a picture of me now?"

"Of course, Secretary Liu, we're not busy today." Jia stood up, knocking the pipe on his palm, and turned to the studio.

"No, not there." Liu explained that he wanted to have a photograph taken of the wound on his bottom, so there was no need for the tall camera and they had better do it in a quiet place.

Unfortunately, the shop's miniature Seagull camera had been sent to Dalian City for repair. They had no choice but to use the tall camera. Jia called over the receptionist, a pallid girl with two tiny brushes of hair behind her ears, and told her to stand at the door of the studio and allow nobody to enter. Then in the heat of the intense lights, Liu ascended the platform, which was used for family or group pictures, to raise his behind to the level of the lens. He was facing the backdrop, an oil painting of a vast landscape filled with terraced fields, in which red flags were flying here and there and midget human figures were working with picks and shovels and carrying baskets loaded with soil. He unbuckled his pants and let them drop over his feet. Turning a little, he kept his right hip toward the camera. His hand held up the leg opening of his red shorts; the wound was displayed above the gluteal fold.

"Goodness, it's black! Is it a dog bite?" Jia asked while turning to the camera.

"No, a man bite," Liu said with his teeth gritted.

"How did it happen?"

"Shao Bin, the son of a turtle, early this morning he went to break up the conference. We tried to stop him, and he went wild and turned on me."

Chuckling, Jia went behind the camera and covered himself with the cloth, saying, "A little bit to your left, that's good."

The photograph taken, Liu buckled up his pants and followed Jia out of the studio. The girl looked at him with a knowing smirk on her face, her eyes rolling. Liu smiled back, then turned to the photographer. "Old Jia, can you make it express? I need five pictures as soon as possible."

"I'll do my best," Jia said in a nasal voice. "At the latest, they'll be ready the day after tomorrow. All right?"

"Good, thanks." Liu turned to the girl. "How much?"

"One twenty-eight."

He paid and went out. But before crossing the granite slabs over the gutter to get to the street, he remembered something and returned to the photo shop. At the sight of him, the girl tittered and sniffled.

"I need a receipt," Liu said.

"Sure." She kept her head low.

While she was writing the receipt, Liu went into the darkroom, in which Jia was coloring a photograph with a little brush. Liu said, "Old Jia, I forgot something very important."

"What?" Jia stood up, brush in hand.

"I want you to put the date on the pictures. Today's June thirtieth."

"I can do that. No problem." Jia's smile revealed a gold molar.

On his way to the Commune Guesthouse, where the conference attendees were to eat a six-course lunch, Liu felt that this time he had caught Shao Bin. He would publicize this incident across the whole county and make him notorious as a mad, man-biting dog. Yes, he was going to heat up the water and boil this turtle alive.

Ten

AFTER LIU GOT THE PHOTOGRAPHS, a general meeting was held in the plant. Since everybody had heard of the incident in the commune's theater, the attendance was unprecedented; never had the dining hall been so full. About a dozen men were sitting on the windowsills.

Director Ma first described how Bin had bitten Secretary Liu. Next he announced that Bin was temporarily dismissed from his work, so that he could have time to write his self-criticism and self-examination. Hearing this, some men booed, because they thought Bin was lucky to have a few days off.

Then Liu took over and addressed the audience. "Comrades, I once observed that Shao Bin had mental trouble. What happened two days ago has proved my point. You all know how important that methane conference was to our commune, but Shao Bin was so crazy he went there to spoil all the work we had done for it. Director Ma and I stopped him in time and tried to persuade him to leave. He wouldn't listen. As we were taking him out, he turned wild and bit my butt." Unconsciously Liu touched his behind with his right hand as though the wound had been inflicted just now.

Too outraged to stand it any more, Bin jumped up and yelled, "If you didn't kick my privates, how could I bite you! If you didn't sit on my face, how could my mouth reach your stinking ass!"

Some of the audience laughed.

"Who kicked your balls?" Liu asked and looked bewildered, as if he had never heard of such a thing.

The laughter grew louder.

"You, you broke my private parts!" Bin was choking with anger and truly believed it was Liu, not Ma, who had hurt him.

"I did?" Liu smiled contemptuously, his eyes half closed. "You've lost your mind. Show us how broken your balls are, anyway."

A burst of laughter filled the room as Bin turned red to the neck. "Shameless snake!" he cursed and sat down.

"Watch your language, Comrade Shao Bin," Liu said. "We're all rational adults, aren't we? We are here to discuss the problem and not to call each other names." He took a wallet out of his pocket, opened it, and raised it to the audience, displaying the photograph of a dark wound. "Here's my butt. Comrade Shao Bin, this isn't a dog bite, is it? Your teeth marks are here. It's ironclad evidence, as solid as a mountain, and with the date on it too." He took the picture out of the cellophane sleeve and slammed it on the table. "I leave it here for everybody to see after the meeting. Shao Bin, you said I broke your balls. Where are your balls? Show us the evidence if you have any."

Liu looked so serious that nobody dared make a noise, though quite a few people tried hard to hold back their laughter. On the verge of tears, Bin stood up and rushed away to the door, shouting back, "You're worse than landowners and capitalists! More pernicious than a counterrevolutionary."

That brought out an explosion of laughter; Bin stormed out of the meeting.

He didn't write a word of self-criticism. Instead, he spent the following days painting plum blossoms and copying stone inscriptions from the Han Dynasty. He had always aspired to possess that kind of ancient simplicity and solidity in his calligraphy. To some degree, he felt happy to be able to practice his arts again. During the day Shanshan was at the nursery school of the department store, so he was alone at home, painting, writing, and humming at will until four o'clock, when he would cook dinner for his family.

Peace and joy, however, were temporary. A few days later the leaders sent Huang Dongfang over to see how much self-criticism Bin had written. Realizing he had done nothing, they ordered him back to work; so he returned to the plant.

Despite his calm appearance, Bin was filled with anxiety. He knew that soon the admission letter would come to the plant, and that the school would request his file and a current evaluation of his moral character, working habits, and lifestyle. This would give the leaders an opportunity to stop him again. They didn't even have to do anything — just withholding his file would be enough to spoil the whole thing. On the other hand, the leaders couldn't hold him back without facing some public pressure, because the admission would surely become known in town. In over twenty years only one boy and two girls in the commune had passed the exams and entered college. People would be impressed this time and say, "Shao Bin is a chosen scholar now. He's leaving for the provincial capital and to be a big official there someday. Who could tell a golden phoenix was hatched in a henhouse? Now whoever is his enemy must be careful, and he will come back someday and have them punished."

So far Bin dared not tell anybody about the admission; he had made Meilan promise that she wouldn't breathe a word. He understood happiness was a private thing and couldn't be shared with others. In addition, he didn't want the leaders to know of the admission before the official letter arrived. If it came, he preferred it to come like thunder, to strike them dumb. Had they heard of the admission beforehand, they would have had time to calculate their moves. This would have left him little time to work on them.

He was unsure how to bring them around; too much enmity had built up recently. He dared not seek advice from anybody in town, because that would be similar to broadcasting the secret. Besides, he had no close friend here.

Having thought about the matter for several days, he decided to ask Yen Fu's opinion, since Yen lived far away. By the time the secret spread from Gold County and reached Dismount Fort, the university's letter would have arrived at the plant.

He wrote to Yen with a fountain pen. Because Yen knew his calligraphy well, there was no need for a brush. The letter went:

July 12

My Dear Brother Yen:

Having not seen you for almost two months, I miss you day and night. How are you? Have you done some good paintings lately?

I am having a terrible time. Two weeks ago I was informed by the Provincial Teachers University that they would admit me as a special student-artist. Then I was beaten black and blue by Liu Shu and Ma Gong. Liu kicked my private parts and sat on my face to smother me.

I don't want to avenge my suffering now, since going to college is more important. I want to leave this madhouse and get a good education in Shenyang City. Brother Yen, this is my last opportunity. It seems that the leaders, including Yang Chen, are unlikely to let me go. What should I do? You have seen the situation here and may have a better idea — I am inside the mountain and can't see the whole mountain. Please give me some advice. Your words are always as precious as gold.

Take good care of yourself.

Shake hands,
Words of Your Brother:
Shao Bin

After putting the letter into a small envelope, he couldn't find the glue bottle. So he sealed it with a few grains of cooked rice. When he went to the nursery school to fetch his daughter, he took the letter with him; the post office was on the way.

Three days later, Bin received a note from the Provincial College Examination Committee. It informed him of his exam results: Math — 18; Politics — 73; Language and Literature — 64. He was so embarrassed by the note that he used it in the latrine. He didn't even mention it to his wife. He was afraid that the plant might get such a note as well. If so, the leaders would definitely make good use of it.

Yen's letter came the next afternoon. He advised Bin to remain calm and patient, biding his time. "Brother

Shao," he wrote, "you must be able to endure; otherwise you will lose the opportunity. Don't talk back or argue with them. Just keep quiet." Yen also suggested that between the two leaders Ma seemed less wicked, so Bin should work on Ma, trying to bring him around first. Meanwhile, Yen would find someone in the county town who knew Secretary Yang well, to persuade him. Once Yang and Ma agreed to let Bin go, Liu would have to concede.

Meilan and Bin thought Yen's advice sound and feasible; they decided to work on Ma without delay.

After supper, they left Shanshan with the salesgirls who lived next door and set out for Ma's. Bin rode his National Defense bicycle, Meilan sitting on its carrier. Coming toward the plant, he saw in the distance the houses in Workers' Park lined up neatly, the red tiles, wet with rain, glistening in the setting sun, and the sycamores beside the houses already leafy with small crowns. Again the sight of the compound kindled his anger, but he forced himself to remain unperturbed. He kept saying to himself, a strong man must be able to stoop and stand up according to circumstances. Housing is something outside yourself and shouldn't be valued too much.

Without Bin's knowledge, that afternoon the official news of his admission had arrived. It indeed came like thunder and blew up the leaders' plan to make a jackass of him in the eyes of the plant. Shao Bin had done it again!

Whatever you called him, a lunatic or a mad dog, you couldn't deny he was bursting with talent and energy and was a scholar by nature. With only five years' education, he had tackled those difficult exams and got admitted to a college, whereas every one of the commune's three hundred high-school graduates had flunked the exams this year. Who could deny that Shao Bin had an extraordinary mind?

The leaders, especially Ma, felt they should have let Bin do the propaganda work; such a conciliatory gesture on their part could have prevented the hostility between Bin and them from mounting up.

"You know what," Ma said to Liu on their way to Workers' Park, "we should've made better use of this odd man and given him an apartment last year."

"Yes, but it's too late now," Liu said thoughtfully. "He's already our deadly enemy. From now on, we must be very careful when dealing with him, or he'll capsize our boat. Who could foretell he'd grow into such a big fish?"

Ma made no further comment and parted company with Liu. He and his wife had saved four thousand yuan for their youngest daughter's college education, but year after year the girl failed the exams. Shao Bin, this wizard of a fitter, had made it with only two weeks' preparation. What could you say? You had to admit he was a tremendous learner at least. In his heart Ma couldn't help but respect Bin. It seemed there was simply no way to stop this weird fellow, and sooner or later he would become somebody.

At dinner Ma told his wife of the news. Mrs. Ma was amazed and upset at the same time, because two days ago they had been informed that their daughter was thirty points below the admission standard. This meant they would have to send her to the preparatory school in Gold County again the next year.

"How come it was so easy for him?" she asked her husband, chewing spinach.

"Beats me."

"You know, this will be big news in town. Are you going to let him go?" Her bulbous nose was wet with beads of perspiration.

"I don't know. Liu Shu and I haven't talked about it yet."

"I think you should let him go this time. If you don't, he'll remember you for the rest of his life. He'll take more revenge. Who wouldn't?" She thrust a spoon of stewed potatoes into the mouth of their two-year-old grandson, who was sitting in her lap.

Ma didn't say another word and kept eating his corn porridge. It was his principle that his wife shouldn't interfere with his work. He picked up a fried loach with his chopsticks and sipped the sorghum liquor from his cup. Though he tried not to think of the admission for the moment, his wife's words were sinking in. He had five children and a grandson and two granddaughters; for them he had better accumulate some virtuous deeds, so that people would treat them well after he left this world. Shao Bin would ruin them if he hurt him too much.

The moment the Mas finished dinner, Bin and Meilan arrived. Mrs. Ma poured them each a cup of jasmine tea and then went to the kitchen to do the dishes. Bin was shocked that the leaders had heard of the admission. Ma told him the letter hadn't been discussed yet. Bin begged him to raise his noble hands just this once and let him go; Ma said that he was not inclined to keep him here and that the admission was also an honor to the plant.

To a certain extent Ma felt for Bin, because he had hit his crotch in the theater, even though Bin thought it was Liu who had done that. "I'll talk with Secretary Liu," said Ma. "We'll let you know of our decision soon." He waved his cigarette, a skein of smoke encircling his hairy wrist.

"Thank you, Director Ma," the couple said in unison.

"Young Shao, let me give you a piece of advice. You should learn to be modest and prudent. One always loses by being proud and gains by being modest." Ma was referring to an instruction from Chairman Mao.

"Yes, I will remember that," Bin said and grinned.

Ma then asked him what textbooks were more useful for the exams. Hesitating for a second, Bin told him he had used the set published by Jilin University. Ma made a mental note to tell his daughter to look into those books.

As Mrs. Ma stepped in, wiping her hands on a towel, Meilan opened her handbag and took out four green apples. "These're for the kid," she said, shyly avoiding Mrs. Ma's eyes. She handed one of them to the baby boy, who was playing with a toy tank on the floor. He looked at the apple but didn't touch it.

"No, we have a lot of fruit," Mrs. Ma said, trying to put the apples back into the handbag.

Meilan stuck the bag under her own arm and said, "Just for the kid, Aunt. They're Indian Green."

Bin didn't want to stay long, he was afraid of being seen by others, so the Shaos took their leave.

After they left, Ma's face sank; he was not pleased with the apples. "What a bookworm," he said to his wife when the young couple were out of earshot. "He doesn't even know how to give a gift. Just four apples, crazy." He tapped his cigarette on the rim of an empty honey jar he used as an ashtray.

He got to his feet and stretched his hands, yawning. With the apples in his jacket pockets, two on each side, he left for Liu's to discuss the college admission.

Bin was working at a welding machine the next morning when Hsiao tapped his shoulder and told him that the plant's leaders wanted him to attend a family-planning meeting in the union office at four in the afternoon. Bin was puzzled, because Meilan and he hadn't done anything violating the one-child policy. He guessed that perhaps he was being invited to help enforce the policy. If so, this wasn't a good sign; in the normal course of events, if he was going to leave the plant soon he shouldn't be assigned any official role. Another thought unnerved him a great deal, namely that the leaders might know his exam results and meant to use this opportunity to ridicule him.

At four, in the union office, all the heads of the workshops and offices were present, in addition to the women representatives and the four workers who had second-born babies. In total, about thirty people sat around six long desks grouped together. Bin took a seat at a corner of a desk.

The union chairman, Bao, started by reporting on the situation of family planning in the plant. He was almost illiterate and couldn't speak well, so in a halting tone he was reading out the report prepared for him by his assistant. He declared that the plant had intended to become a model of implementing the family-planning policy, but four second-born babies this year had spoiled the plan. The Third Workshop alone had three second-borns.

After Bao was done with the report, Secretary Liu stood up and announced that all those with second-born babies would lose a whole year's bonus and wouldn't get a raise for two years. Groans came from around the table.

"I'm not coldhearted, comrades," Liu said. "The punishment for a second-born is clearly written in the most recent document. We have no choice but to implement it, unless you can prove that your firstborn is retarded or from a previous marriage." He stretched out his right hand, wiggling his fingers, as though inviting somebody to stand up and argue with him. No one moved except Ma.

Ma rose to his feet and waved to Nina, who was sitting in the next room. She came in, carrying a large string bag of National Glory apples with both hands, and put the fruit on the desk in front of Liu; then she went and sat down on a chair by the door. She gave Bin a contemptuous stare, her lips in a pout. At the sight of the red apples, Bin's heart began kicking; he knew something was wrong. Liu squinted at him and smiled with his mustache twitching.

"Comrades," Liu said loudly, "let me announce another decision here. Yesterday afternoon we received a letter from the Provincial Teachers University. It says they might admit Shao Bin to their Fine Arts Department and asks us, the plant's leaders, to give an evaluation of him and the permission for him to leave. Before we reached a decision, yesterday evening Shao Bin and his wife went to Director Ma's home with this gift." Liu lifted the thirty-odd apples and dropped them on the desk with a thump. "And he begged Director Ma to give him the permission to go. Too late, I say. You can't embrace the Buddha's feet only in your hour of need, when for years you've never bothered to burn a joss stick or kowtow to him."

Liu turned to Bin and kept on. "Shao Bin, you've painted cartoons about us and made us look like corrupt officials. But why do *you* practice corruption shamelessly, bribing a revolutionary cadre? Let me tell you this now: We're not that cheap; a bag of apples won't buy us off." He lifted the string bag again. Before he put it down, a camera flashed at him; as arranged, Dongfang had brought his camera to the meeting.

Some people smirked, while a few sighed, shaking their heads. "Comrades," Liu resumed, "three weeks ago Shao Bin bit my butt. Now he's tried to bribe Director Ma. I used to think he was merely a lunatic, suffering from schizophrenia or something, but the bribe has made me change my mind. He must have a moral problem too. Therefore this morning our Party Committee sent out a letter, together with the photos of my wound and these apples as two samples of his 'work,' to the university and informed them that we wouldn't agree about their decision and wouldn't provide Shao Bin's file for them. In short, he's not qualified to go to college, neither mentally nor morally."

Bin broke out wailing, which scared the people around him. He yelled, "I screw your ancestors! You wait and see, I'll dump your grandsons into a well!"

The last sentence horrified Liu and Ma, because each had only one grandson, a single seedling of the entire family, and Bin had said clearly, "grandsons," meaning both of theirs. Though he might be bluffing, a desperate madman like him could do anything. If he did that, their family lines would be cut. Now they doubted whether they had done a wise thing by sending out the letter of refusal so soon. It seemed they had pressed Bin too hard without giving him a way out. Naturally he had exploded. Ma couldn't help glaring at Liu, who had convinced him that they had best hold Bin back; the night before, Ma had been inclined to let him leave.

For a good two minutes neither Liu nor Ma knew what to do; they stood there whispering to each other and scratching their scalps and necks, while Bin was weeping and sniffling, his face buried in his arms on the desk. The meeting turned chaotic. Some people said the leaders should let Bin go; they could deduct his bonus and even beat him, but stopping him from entering college was way too much; by doing so, they ruined his whole life. If there was no hope left, who wouldn't go berserk? Some said the leaders had promised to support whoever took the entrance exams, and now Bin was admitted, which was an event that should be celebrated in the plant, why didn't they keep their word? Who would try again the next year? Who would believe them in the future? Liu and Ma as leaders were too nearsighted and narrow-minded. As for the bag of apples, Bin must have done it in desperation; it was perfectly understandable if you were utterly confused and frightened and had no idea what to do. However, those who had always hated this pseudo-scholar remained silent, smirking.

Finally Director Ma clapped his hands and declared the meeting was over.

"Oh, I'm sorry," Meilan moaned after Bin told her what the leaders had done. "I thought the Mas didn't have Indian apples. I didn't mean to bribe him."

"Why didn't you tell me beforehand?" He was angry and had planned to slap her.

"I'm sorry. I thought you'd be too stubborn to allow me." She began weeping, blaming herself for having ruined his future. Her tears softened him.

Instead of questioning her further, he handed her a wet towel. He felt that in a way he himself was to blame too. He had seen her handbag bulging strangely but hadn't asked what was inside; he had been too careless, knowing she was a sort of oddball. Yet all in all, it was neither her fault nor his. Those hoodlums just wanted to do him in and had made a pond out of a pee puddle. It doesn't matter if something bad has happened; what matters is the person who takes advantage of it. Wicked people will create misfortune for you.

That night he wrote to Yen and told him that everything was gone. The university would surely accept the official statement from the plant and drop him. He swore he would avenge this injustice someday, but for the time being he had to get out of here. Obviously the leaders were set on broiling him alive. He felt as though his heart would explode with rage at any moment. "A bomb," he wrote, "my heart is like an atomic bomb, eager to blast everything." He knew he might grab hold of Liu's and Ma's grandsons and hurt the children badly if more pressure was put on him. At the end of the letter, he begged Yen, "Help your older brother, please!"

It was a long letter, six pages written with a pen. After completing it, he was too exhausted to climb onto the bed; he remained at the desk and let his head rest in the crook of his arm. In no time a thread of saliva began dribbling from the corner of his mouth. As he was snoring away, a soft sound whistled in his nose.

He slept this way until daybreak.

Eleven

On thursday evening a young man came to visit Bin. He introduced himself as Song Zhi, a reporter and a colleague of Yen's at the newspaper *Environment.* He was bareheaded and wore an old army uniform; one of the knees of his pants was covered with a rectangular patch that looked brand new. He said Yen had told Bin's story to the editorial staff, and everybody had felt outraged by Liu's and Ma's abuse of power. So the editor in chief, Jiang Ping, sent him over to investigate and report on the case.

Bin was impressed by Song, who not only had good manners but also looked handsome, with a square face, a straight nose, large, sparkling eyes, and broad shoulders. He felt Song was a trustworthy man who seemed to exude compassion.

They talked over tea and melons. Outside the window, the moon was wavering above the aspen crowns like a silver sickle slicing strips of clouds. Katydids were chirping away, and a young male voice was singing Peking opera in a neighboring courtyard.

Bin was talking about how evil Liu and Ma were while Song was writing down his words in a notebook. He went on for about twenty minutes; then he stopped to declare loudly, "They're both thugs and bandits without any Communist conscience. I often wonder if they are from reactionary families; otherwise, where on earth could they have got such wicked minds? One night I dreamed Liu Shu was a fat landlord who died of thousands of cuts, hacked to pieces by revolutionary masses. In any case, we must have these vermin kicked out of the Party." He kept slapping his thigh.

"Don't be too emotional, Comrade Old Shao. Just tell me the facts," said Song.

At that, Bin swallowed a gulp of tea to calm himself down. He remembered he himself wasn't a Party member yet, though he had applied for membership many times. So he had better not discuss how the Party should punish the two leaders.

"Say everything clearly to Young Song," Meilan told Bin, "or how can he expose them?"

Patiently Song was writing. Having controlled his anger, Bin continued to talk about the injustice in the housing assignment, and then about the leaders' persecuting him for the works of art he had published. He took out the cartoons about housing and holiday bribery and gave Song a copy of each to take back as evidence.

After that, he described Secretary Yang's role in these incidents, asserting that it was because Yang was behind the scenes that Liu and Ma dared to torture him so flagrantly. They always served Yang as though he were their grandfather; in return, Yang would cover up for them whatever crimes they committed. Their control was so tight that this commune was simply an independent empire, into which even a needle couldn't find its way. To conclude, Bin said, "All the officials here are rotten. There isn't a clean, honest one to whom you can report your thoughts."

Song wrote that down too; by now he was also incensed by the leaders' evildoing.

After Bin put the kettle back on the self-made electric stove — a coil of tungsten wire embedded in a large brick — he began to talk about how Liu had kicked his private parts. "I went to the theater to see if Vice Governor Long had come. I had once shaken hands with him in the provincial capital, you know. But Liu and Ma accused me of disrupting the conference. Without warning they attacked me. Liu kicked me right here, and I dropped flat on the floor." He pointed at his groin and continued, "I was so hurt I couldn't get up, but they pinched my cheeks and twisted my ears to drag me up. I couldn't move; I almost fainted. Then Liu Shu dropped his big ass on my face and said, 'I'm smothering you to death on the spot.' He weighs almost two hundred pounds, you know. My glasses were smashed, I couldn't breathe, and the bridge of my nose was about to snap. So I opened my mouth and gave him a bite, just driven by the instinct for survival."

Song almost tittered and asked, "Then what happened?"

"Liu was so brazen he took a photo of his ass and showed the bite to everyone, saying I had attacked him from behind for no reason at all, and this proved that I had a mental disorder. You see what a goddamn liar he is."

"Did you do anything to clarify the case?"

"What could I do? It's obvious that if I had attacked him I wouldn't have chosen his stinking ass to bite, would I?"

"No."

"He's the Party secretary, with a bigger mouth that can outshout mine. Besides, I can't take a photo of my balls and publicize it, can I? He's low, but I mustn't be lower, you know."

"True, that's very true." Song nodded, and his black fountain pen kept writing.

Meilan and Shanshan had by now fallen asleep with their clothes on, a pink toweling blanket covering them both. Time and again Meilan murmured something, smiling. It was getting late, almost ten-thirty, and Song hadn't heard everything yet, so they decided to resume their talk the next evening. In the meantime, Song would visit the plant, ideally catching a glimpse of Liu and Ma, so that when he wrote the article he would have a better grip on the ambience and the characters. After Bin described to him how to get to the plant and where the leaders' offices were, Song drank up the last drops of tea, put the notebook into his pocket, and took his leave.

The night turned cloudy, and a dog in the neighborhood began yapping. In the distance a tractor was passing and blaring its horn, while soundless lightning streaked across the northern sky.

For some reason Bin was possessed by a mysterious joy that hadn't come to him for a long time. He felt fortunate to be acquainted with a cultured young man like Song. He was so excited, he took out his brushes and ink slab; then a giddy feeling came over him, and he knew he had to paint something right now. Grasping his thick hair, he was thinking hard of a subject.

Yes, he would paint a piece for Song, to express his gratitude and trust. With his hollowed palm he scooped some water from the washbasin behind the door and put it into the ink slab. He then set about grinding the ink stick; his mind was busy working on a subject. A few minutes later he was certain what to do.

He dipped a large brush into the ink, let it get saturated, then started to draw. After a few strokes the stalwart figure of Zhong Kui, the legendary devil executioner, took shape on the paper. Bin used the technique of splash-ink to give him a long, thick beard, which seemed to be fluttering with anger. His loose-fitting robe was also flapping, as though a steady breeze was blowing from one side. His left hand grasped a list of devils' names, while his right carried a huge crescent sword, whose broad blade slanted before his knee. The sole of his left boot was raised as if to trample a devil in front of him.

Viewing Zhong Kui's square face for a moment, Bin put two dots as a pair of pupils into the eye sockets he had already drawn. It was too bad the size of the devils' list couldn't be larger, or he would have written Liu Shu and Ma Gong on it. He laid down the brush and picked up a small one. After letting it absorb enough ink, he wrote in a vertical line at the right side: "Execute the Devils." Beneath the title, he inscribed in cursive: "For Comrade Song Zhi. Please Point Out My Inadequacies." Then he pressed his oblong seal beside the inscription.

"My, my," he murmured, amazed by the bold piece of work. His eyes blurred with joyful tears. It seemed to him that this was his masterpiece; he found the whole painting marked by an august aura and radiating an upright spirit. Though no devil was present in the scene, one could feel that the execution was about to take place. Zhong Kui's colossal figure would definitely paralyze any devil in his presence before he captured and beheaded it. "Damn, what a piece," Bin mumbled, licking his mustache.

He couldn't help wondering why for all these years he had studied and worked hard, only intending to produce a piece like this, and he had never succeeded, but all of a sudden he had made it with so much ease, strength, and mastery, as though he had practiced drawing this very piece for decades. A happy mood shouldn't be the answer, because there had been a lot of shadows in his mind. He recalled the process of creating it, and felt as if something had just gushed out of his chest and splashed onto the paper. What was that thing bottled up in him? He figured it must have been the pain and suffering he had gone through recently. He remembered that when he was drawing the sword, the brushstrokes had been so ferocious that he had paused to see whether he had poked a hole through the paper. So it was the misery and rage that had driven the brush to make such a breakthrough in his art. He realized anger was also a source of power, which the artist ought to convert into creative energy.

Then he felt reluctant to present this piece to Song. Heaven knew when he could accomplish such a work again. On second thought, he decided to let it go, since he had already inscribed the dedication; besides, by coming here to help him, Song had contributed to its creation. You shouldn't be too small-minded, Bin warned himself.

The next morning Bin came across Song in front of the office building in the plant. They glanced at each other without exchanging greetings, because they needed to appear to others as strangers in order to forestall the leaders' suspicion.

As Song and Bin were passing each other, Liu happened to come out of his office, descending the stairs.

"Good morning, Secretary Liu Shu," Bin shouted from a distance of fifty yards, waving as though they had been old friends. He did this for Song, to identify Liu for him; Song turned to look at the stocky leader.

Apparently Bin's warm greeting frightened Liu. He halted on the stairs, speechless and bulgy-eyed, then turned around and hurried back toward his office. Bin saw Liu's surprised face, and he gave a hearty laugh, swaggering away. The laugh shook Liu's heart.

God knew what made that lunatic so happy today. Something must have been going on. Suddenly Liu remembered his grandson, and cold sweat broke out in his armpits. He was in the middle of a meeting and couldn't go home, so he hastened to Finance and begged Nina, almost with tears, to go tell his wife to take the boy out of the plant's childcare center and watch him carefully at home today. Damn this mad dog Shao Bin! If only they could have slammed him into jail.

The fear on Liu's face pleased Bin a lot. While filing a brass faucet in Maintenance, he couldn't help humming a folk song. His fellow workers asked him why he was so different this morning. He told them he had had an auspicious dream the night before, with whales and a boat that carried him into the blue ocean. Asked further, he wouldn't explain what this meant but kept smiling mysteriously. "What a superstitious bookworm," they said behind his back. At lunch he bought a good dish — fried tofu cubes mixed with pork and leeks — and also a mug of beer.

He felt nobody in the world could subdue him after he had painted "Execute the Devils," which ought to be a masterpiece. Probably this work would survive him and become a sought-after treasure, passing through generations to posterity. It was too bad that Song would have it; otherwise he would have sent it to the National Gallery in Beijing. If they accepted it, he might be able to go to a university, not as a student but as a lecturer or a professor, just like the cobbler who had recently been invited to teach math at a major university on the strength of his inventing a method of rapid calculation.

In the evening Song came again. Bin talked about the leaders' breaking their promise to let him go to college and then about Liu's lifestyle. He insisted that somebody had seen Liu and Nina lying in each other's arms on the bank of the reservoir near Quarry Village, and that they went to the waterside every Sunday afternoon. On their way there Liu often bought her grapes, or sweetmeats, or boiled periwinkles, or steamed mantis shrimps. Bin defined the affair thus: "Liu Shu purchases her thighs with power. That's why Hou Nina was given a new apartment and got a raise each year."

After their talk, Bin took out "Execute the Devils." Song looked excited by the painting and said, "Comrade Old Shao, thank you for trusting us."

His words puzzled Bin. Bin said, "I painted this for you, to express my gratitude, yes, also my trust."

"We'll cherish it and hang it in our editorial office." Song rolled the painting up and put it under his arm. He slung his duffel onto his back, getting ready to leave for the ten o'clock train.

They shook hands and said good-bye.

Bin felt mortified by the rough way Song had handled the painting. It seemed Song took it as something like a poster and obviously wouldn't mind sharing it with anyone. Now Bin began to doubt Song's character; at least he no longer took him for a good friend. You shouldn't play the lute to a water buffalo, he said to himself. Without doubt Song was ignorant of the fine arts, unable to appreciate real work.

Twelve

HAVING READ SONG'S report on Bin's case, Jiang Ping, the editor in chief of *Environment,* felt that after minor revisions he should publish it. Though the newspaper was designed mainly to bring natural environmental issues to people's awareness, it would be better if once in a while it published something about the social environment — to reduce moral and cultural pollution.

Two weeks later the report came out on the front page of *Environment* with the title "The Legend of Shao Bin." It consisted of four long sections: first, "A Conscientious Artist"; second, "Persecutions After Two Cartoons"; third, "In the Face of the Abuse of Power"; fourth, "A Cry of Blood and Justice." In addition to the thirty-five hundred words, a photograph of Bin, three inches by two, was printed in the first section, and the cartoons about housing and bribery appeared in the middle of the article. There were also the prints of two seals carved by Bin in the Worm Style; one said, "Eliminate the Wicked and Enhance the Good," and the other, "Justice Will Prevail." The sentences in the article were trenchant, emotional, now and then invigorated by a pair of exclamation marks. Never had *Environment* looked so lively.

The minute the newspaper came off the press, Yen sent two copies to Bin by the express mail.

On reading the article Bin burst into tears, which scared his daughter. She dropped her bottle and ran out of the room, shouting, "Mommy, Daddy's crying."

Meilan rushed in with an iron ladle in her hand. Seeing the half-filled bottle lying on the dirt floor, she became angry, about to yell at Bin. But he smiled and handed her a copy of the newspaper, saying, "I got them! Caught them all in one net."

She took the paper and hurried back to the kerosene stove, on which a wok of celery and potato slivers was sizzling. She left in the room an aromatic puff of scallion, fried with soy sauce.

To Bin, the best feature of the article was its broad scope — no relevant detail was left out. There were twelve places where Secretary Yang's name was mentioned. At one point, the author even questioned him directly: "As the head of the commune, you didn't make any effort to correct the wrong done by Liu and Ma, but instead you connived with them. Where is the principled stand of a Communist? How could you forget and maltreat the people who put the power in your hands? We advise Comrade Yang Chen to think this over."

Bin perused those powerful sentences several times and was convinced that whoever read the article would feel that the indignation was honest and justified. This time Secretary Yang could not feign innocence and remain behind the scenes; he had to face his crimes and pay for them.

After supper Bin cycled to Bank Street and stuck the article, with twelve thumbtacks, to the propaganda board in front of the Commune Administration. From there he went directly to the plant to post the other copy. It was too bad that Yen had mailed him just two copies; if only he could have kept one for his own records.

When Bin arrived at work the next morning, the newspaper had vanished from the notice board. At first he was outraged, but seeing some workers grin at him knowingly, he felt a little comforted. One of them said, "Bin, you looked so handsome in the paper, like an eighteen-year-old."

Another asked, "Did you get paid for the article? How much a word?"

What a silly question. Bin didn't bother to answer, reluctant to admit he wasn't the author and had got no pay for the writing.

Strangely, neither Liu nor Ma looked scared when they came to the workshop to question Bin. Liu told him bluntly in the presence of his fellow workers, "You've done enough; this is the end. We'll sue you for libel, and our commune will sue you too!"

"Yes," Ma said. "You think you're good at screwing people over, but this time you screwed your own asshole."

"Tell us who wrote the article," Liu ordered.

Bin kept silent. Their words unnerved him, so he said he had to go to the latrine and would be back in just a minute to answer their questions. He put a handful of cotter pins on the workbench, held his sides with both hands as though suffering from enteritis, and left. Once outside, he fled to the Second Workshop, fearing the leaders would rough him up.

In Maintenance, Liu and Ma, having waited for twenty minutes, were cursing Bin loudly. "Next time," Liu said, "we'll tie him to a bench when we question him. Even if he messes his pants we won't let him go."

Ever since the article was published, the telephone in the editorial office of *Environment* had been ringing continually. Many people called to relate similar stories of their own and begged the editors to report them; at the same time, some officials called and claimed that the article was full of distortions and that the editors must be answerable for the consequences. The Bureau of Environmental Protection of Gold County, which sponsored the newspaper, dispatched two cadres, with a policeman, to the editorial office to investigate the case. In addition, the leaders summoned Jiang Ping to the bureau and rebuked him. They reminded him that the newspaper was a public mouthpiece, not a means for venting private malice and causing social disturbances. Jiang, however, was too stubborn to admit he had done anything wrong and insisted that reporting evil winds didn't contradict the aim of the newspaper, because the title *Environment* ought to include both the natural and the social. Nonetheless, his superiors ordered him to write out a self-criticism and make a detailed report on the process of the article's publication.

The pressure from higher authorities was too much for the bureau to bear. The County Party Committee, the People's Congress, and the Administration all had demanded that the bureau investigate the case and criticize the editor in chief for distorting the facts and for the damage the article had done to the image of the Party leaders in the countryside.

Within a week the bureau issued a document, taking these measures:

1. Stop shipping out the newspaper at once.
2. The editor in chief, Comrade Jiang Ping, must examine and find out the subjective cause of this mistake. He must turn in his self-criticism as soon as possible.
3. All the editorial staff must learn a serious lesson from this mistake and ensure that it will not happen again.
4. The bureau will administer the final punishment according to Jiang Ping's attitude and the result of the current investigation.

Still, Jiang believed that what he had done was within the power of his position and that there was no violation of any rule, so he refused to write a self-criticism. He asserted to the bureau's leaders that to voice the grievance of an underdog was a common practice in journalism. Every one of the Party's newspapers had done this again and again; why couldn't *Environment* do the same?

He was not frightened by the petty bureaucrats, because he had relatives in Beijing. If necessary, they could help him lodge a complaint with the State Council.

After questioning Yen and Song, the investigating team took "Execute the Devils" off the wall of the editorial office, saying they would keep it as evidence of Bin's bribing the staff. Jiang argued that he had paid twenty yuan for having the painting mounted and owned a part of it now. They then agreed to "borrow" it for a few weeks.

On the same day the team went to Dismount Fort by jeep to talk with the slandered cadres. Secretary Yang received them with a wry face, as though he had a pain in his chest. He denied knowing anything about Shao Bin and insisted that he had been sniped at for an unknown reason. He implored the team to discover the man behind Bin, because it was unlikely that an obscure worker alone would be so bold and so determined to get at him, as if there were a long-standing feud between their clans. Yang suspected that his enemy Ding Liang, the commune's chairman, had masterminded both the scurrilous article and the disruption of the election. Yang felt Bin was nothing but a gun loaded by Ding. He had told his assistant, Dong Cai, to ferret out the connection between Bin and the Ding faction, but so far Dong hadn't come up with any concrete evidence.

The investigating team assured Yang that they would look into the matter in a professional way. Then they went to the Harvest Fertilizer Plant and met with Liu and Ma. The two leaders asserted that Bin was a lunatic and had done everything out of malice and selfish motives. They showed the investigators the photographs of Liu's bitten bottom and of the apples; they emphasized that the only reason the plant hadn't fired Bin was that he suffered from mental trouble and might do something desperate if provoked. Also, they had always pitied him. Without much effort they convinced the team that the article was full of fiction. So the investigators concluded that at most the article was a one-sided story; they presented this conclusion to the bureau.

Two days later, the bureau issued another document, ordering Jiang Ping to leave his position. Since the leaders neither appointed a new editor in chief nor specified how the newspaper should be run in the future, it was obvious the paper was banned and its staff was laid off for the time being. Though still on the bureau's payroll, Jiang, Yen, and Song couldn't believe they had become idle men so suddenly. This idleness was simply beyond their endurance. They wanted to work. Nobody had the right to prevent them from serving the people and the socialist motherland.

The catastrophe, however, created unprecedented solidarity among the editorial staff. For a week they met at Yen's in the evening, discussing how to make their superiors reinstate the newspaper without taking any of them off the board. Yen's mother-in-law was ill, and his wife had gone to her mother's and left the house to him, so Yen's home became the editorial staff's secret office, comfortable and unwatched. After two meetings, they concluded that the most important thing to do now was make the case known to the masses, to exert public pressure on their superiors. They all agreed Bin had to play a key role in publicizing the wrongs, since he was the initial victim and the immediate cause of Jiang's dismissal. Obviously, unless Bin's case was redressed, it would be impossible for them to get rehabilitated. So Yen sent Bin a letter informing him of what had happened and asking him to come to Gold County as soon as possible. "We have to find effective countermeasures," he wrote. "Please come to my house directly after you get off the train."

Reading Yen's letter on his way to the candy shop on Market Street, Bin almost blacked out, and for a good three minutes he held a concrete pole to keep himself from collapsing. The passersby on bicycles looked back at him with wondering eyes while he motioned again and again, assuring them that he was all right and didn't need help. Instead of going to the shop, he turned back and hurried home. Now the whole fleet is sunk, he said to himself; because of me they have all lost their jobs, and the newspaper is gone too. Damn! it's not worth it, the price is too high. They are all ruined.

By instinct he knew it was too late to retreat for self-protection. Besides, if he deserted them now, everyone would curse him, and in the townspeople's eyes he would become a pile of dog feces stinking for decades. There was no way out, so he had to join forces with them. He felt sick and tired as he showed Meilan the letter, telling her of the new development. How he was longing to take a short vacation, to go somewhere away from this mess and turmoil.

To his amazement, Meilan calmly took a ten-yuan note out of her purse and handed it to him, saying, "You must go help your friends." She sounded as though, in addition to his artistic talent, he was also a sort of strategist, capable of turning the tide. He took the money and caught the next train to Gold County.

Without difficulty Bin found Yen's. He lifted the large iron ring on the gate and clapped it, but no sound came from inside. He knocked again; still there was no response. After waiting a few moments, he pushed the gate open and entered the yard. Two oval flower beds, edged with serrated bricks, spread beneath the granite wall and were filled with tulips, white and yellow. An aquarium with a steel frame sat on a stone table in the middle of the yard, with some tropical fish swimming in it like flying swallows and strings of bubbles rising from the bottom covered with pebbles. To the left was a tiny vegetable garden fenced with twigs, in which cucumbers and kidney beans were hanging on trellises. At the end of the garden, in front of the dark brick house, two peach trees were laden with fruit, and between the trees a hand pump craned over a well.

Seeing the black ceramic tiles on the roof, Bin couldn't help but envy Yen his residence, which had apparently belonged to a rich family in the old China. Yen lives like a landlord, Bin thought.

As he entered the outer room, Bin heard voices talking. A meeting was in full swing, with Song and Yen arguing loudly.

They stopped to greet Bin, then told him that a lengthy letter of complaint had just been composed and that they had been discussing where to send it. Jiang had an aunt in Beijing who was an editor at the journal *Law and Democracy*, so he thought she must know somebody in the State Council and could help them present the letter directly to the Civil Inquiry Department.

Yen disagreed, saying, "China is a huge country, and

that department must receive thousands of letters a day. Ours can't be special by any means. Who knows in what year they will handle our case if we follow the common procedure?"

"That's true," Bin said. "I wrote them half a year ago. So far I haven't heard a word from them."

Jiang batted his round eyes; he was unhappy about what they had said, but on second thought he felt they might be right. Time was crucial here; they couldn't afford to delay even for a month, to say nothing of a few years. What move should they take then? Everybody was racking his brain for an answer.

Bin slapped his knee and said loudly, "Well, why look for the donkey while you're riding him?" He turned to Jiang. "Why not ask your aunt to have it published in *Law and Democracy*? That's an authoritative journal. They published one of my seal prints two years ago. I'm sure any words from Beijing will make the leaders incontinent."

They all laughed and agreed it was a good idea. Song said, "I think we should send somebody to Beijing, to make sure they help us without delay. It will save a lot of time."

"Yes, we must do it immediately," Yen added.

Since none of the editorial staff could leave without arousing their superiors' suspicion, Bin became the only candidate for the trip. In addition, he was the main victim and had to have his own case rectified too, so everybody wanted him to leave for Beijing the next morning, taking the four o'clock train directly from the county town.

"What's the rush?" Bin asked.

They said it was already Tuesday, and the letter of complaint must reach the editorial board of the journal within the week.

Bin didn't mind visiting the capital, but the opportunity had turned up so suddenly he wasn't prepared. So he began explaining the inconvenience. Yet, they all begged him to consider the dismal situation, the improvement of which depended solely on the success of this trip. How could he eat and sleep well while his friends were all in deep water and scorching fire? He was obligated to go. Please, no more dillydallying.

After only ten minutes' persuasion, Bin agreed.

A few problems, however, had to be solved before his departure. First, he couldn't wear his canvas pants, which were work clothes, and plastic sandals to the capital. Look at them, there were a few oil stains on the trouser legs, and one of the sandals had lost its buckle, the lacing belt was stuck between his toes. Second, he had no national grain coupon with him and no money for the train fare. Third, he had to have an official letter, or no place would let him stay overnight and he might be arrested. Fourth, his wife had to learn about this trip as soon as possible; otherwise she might think he had been kidnapped and go to the plant, demanding that the leaders return him to her. Fifth, he had to cover up this trip medically, or else the leaders would know of it and take countermeasures. Sixth, and most important of all, he ought to take a painting or a piece of calligraphy with him as a gift for Jiang's uncle, his aunt's husband, who was a literary scholar. This wasn't a bribe. Every educated Chinese understood that a work of art could be neither eaten nor worn — it had no practical value at all and only showed the artist's cultivation and personality. Presenting someone with a painting was something like a spiritual exchange and was absolutely appropriate and necessary for this occasion. Those cadres on the investigating team were benighted country boors: they took "Execute the Devils" as a bribe only because they were ignorant of the literati's convention.

Jiang said he would go home and get some grain coupons and a hundred yuan for Bin. Because his uncle was a physician in charge at the Country Central Hospital, Song was going to ask the old man to make out a sick-leave certificate for Bin, which Yen would personally take to Dismount Fort the next morning, so that before noon Meilan could have it passed on to Hsiao Peng, the director of Maintenance. As long as she kept people from entering their home, no one would discover Bin wasn't ill. Of course Shanshan had to be careful too, not to let out the secret that her dad wasn't home. As for the official letter, Yen happened to have a blank piece of stationery at home, with their editorial seal on it, so he could fill it out for Bin.

Though Yen found a pair of leather loafers that were Bin's size, no suitable pants were available. The other men were either too bulky or too tall for Bin to wear their clothes. What should they do? Then the thought came to Yen that Bin wasn't much taller than his wife. He went into the inner room, opened the wardrobe, and took out a pair of black slacks for Bin to try on. Bin put them on, the fine silk giving his legs a caressing tingle. Amazingly, they suited him well. "You look like a kung-fu master," Song said. They all laughed.

Indeed, combined with the white, V-necked T-shirt and the loafers whose thick soles added two inches to Bin's height, the slacks made him look natural and rather elegant.

The work of art, however, was difficult. It's common sense that artistic inspiration cannot be summoned. Even though Bin was able to make a piece of calligraphy under the pressure of the moment, it would be impossible to mount it overnight. Yen had quite a few paintings done by himself, but none of them looked good enough for this occasion. Finally, again it was Yen who came up with a solution. Since Bin was a sort of stone epigraphist, why couldn't he carve a seal for Jiang's uncle? One didn't need inspiration for carving a few words on a stone.

What one needed were skills, strength, and artistic cultivation. Yen told them he had several jade stones at home.

Jiang was pleased and said, "Damn you, Yen, your belly is stuffed with ideas; no wonder it's so big. You should be an aide to the provincial governor."

"All right, when you reach that position, don't forget me," Yen said, and slapped his own chest with both hands.

They laughed heartily.

Bin knew it would take him a few hours to complete the carving, but this was the only practicable thing to do. He chose a green jade stone, picked up Yen's tool kit, and went to the inner room, where he would be alone, to concentrate on the work.

After biting his fingertips for a few moments, he decided to engrave Tu Fu's line "Your brush writes, raising wind and rain." It seemed no words were more appropriate as a compliment to Jiang's uncle, a senior editor in a publishing house. Bin wrote out the words in the style of the ancient official script on the face of the seal and then began carving. He felt Yen's knife was not as keen as his own, but it would have to do. Soon his hands were sweaty.

Meanwhile, in the other room Jiang was writing a letter for Bin to carry to his aunt. Song had left for his uncle's to get the sick-leave certificate. In the kitchen Yen was cutting snap beans and pork with which to cook noodles for a midnight snack. Everyone was delightedly busy. The only other time they remembered being as brisk and purposeful was the beginning of the Cultural Revolution, when everybody had fought with a brush at night, writing posters and slogans.

Thirteen

THE TRAIN BOUND FOR BEIJING pulled out at four-ten in the morning. Bin waved goodbye to Yen and Song, who had accompanied him all the way to the station. To avoid being noticed by others, Yen and Song were standing among a score of people beyond the white railings. As the train moved out, Bin's eyes were wet and his nose congested; he was touched by the commitment of these brothers, who had slept only two hours, preparing him for the trip.

Unlike a slow train, which would be so full that even its aisles and vestibules would be occupied by people, piglets, chickens, baskets, and parcels, this was an express train, from Dandong City to Beijing; it didn't stop at small towns and had no unseated passengers. Without difficulty Bin found a window seat. Opposite him sat a young couple, dozing away. The woman's face was resting on the table, her head cloaked in a red jacket, while the man leaned against her, a blue cap covering his face.

Bin looked out the window. Strips of mist were flitting by, and wire poles and mulberry trees were falling away. Green paddies, glimmering and undulating in the breeze, surrounded a village; some chimneys were exhaling smoke; a pair of magpies were flapping on a treetop. Beyond rows of dwarf houses stood a barren, steep hill on which a few gigantic words were built in white rocks: "Grasp Revolution, Promote Production."

Bin closed his eyes and tried to get some sleep, since there would be a busy evening in Beijing and he should appear in high spirits when meeting Jiang's relatives. The music of a Mongolian song was slow and soothing. Soon he dozed off.

Although the place where Jiang's aunt lived wasn't hard to find, it took Bin almost two hours to get there after he alighted from the train, because buses in the capital moved slower than bicycles. Following Jiang's directions, Bin took the No. 103 bus and got off at its terminus — Beijing Zoo. Then he walked west, toward the last glow of the setting sun. After two blocks, he turned south and went along a short boulevard, full of neon lights and Hong Kong music. Having walked along the sidewalk for about five minutes, he saw a group of residential buildings enclosed by a brick wall. According to the map Jiang had drawn, this was the place.

At the entrance to the compound, he was stopped by an old guard, who was bony and entirely bald, and had fat ears. The man read Bin's official letter and told him that Li Peina, Jiang's aunt, lived at 423 in Building 6.

Bin was surprised to see that Peina wasn't an old woman. She was pleasant looking, plump, and in her late forties, just a few years older than her nephew Jiang Ping.

"Come in, Comrade Young Shao," she said tepidly, rubbing her floury hands on her apron. Seeing that he was somewhat amazed by her greeting, she smiled with her round eyes narrowed and said, "I received a telegram from my nephew this afternoon."

Bin followed her in. The skin of her brownish arms reminded him of the bread in a bakery window he had seen a few minutes ago. Her permed hair was slightly gray and covered half her neck. She led him into a large room, where a middle-aged man in black-rimmed glasses was sitting at a desk and reading the *Beijing Evening News.*

"This is my husband," Peina said to Bin.

Sitting in the chair and still keeping his eyes on the newspaper, the man silently stretched up his hand. Bin shook it, feeling it was as soft as a young girl's.

"Have a seat," Peina said, and pointed to a chair by the desk. Bin sat down and looked around. He was amazed to see hundreds of books in Russian on the shelves along the walls.

The man in glasses was still reading.

"He works at the Foreign Literature Publishing House," Peina explained. Bin nodded and noticed the man had shiny, dark hair, in contrast to his face, which was creased like a shriveled gingerroot.

Finally the man put down the newspaper and said in a bass voice, "I'm Chai Hsin. You can call me Old Chai." Seeing Bin's eyes moving along the books, he went on to explain, "I'm a translator of Russian literature, mainly poetry."

Bin was impressed and asked, "Do you translate Pushkin?"

"No. I used to, but now I work on modern Russian poets, particularly Yesenin, whose style I try to learn."

"So you're a poet?" Bin blurted out. He knew Yesenin was a lyric poet, though his knowledge of his poetry was limited to the three poems in the anthology *One Hundred Modern Russian Lyrics.*

Mr. Chai smiled, displaying his tobacco-stained teeth, and said, "Sometimes I write poetry. So you know Yesenin's work?"

"Yes" — Bin nodded — "I like his lyrical style, very touching, so beautiful." Then, with a thumping heart, he recited aloud the lines that had moved him to tears when he had read them three years before:

> Oh, the language of my countrymen
> Is alien to me all at once.
> I am a foreigner in my own town.

Mr. Chai lowered his head, listening, as though bewildered by the Chinese words; then a smile like a crumpled chrysanthemum spread on his face. "I'm damned, that's from 'Soviet Russia'!" He kept shaking his head.

"Yes." Bin felt relieved, because he had forgotten the title of the poem; Mr. Chai had helped him out just in time.

Peina meanwhile poured boiling water into a teapot, muttering, "My nephew never stops making trouble. He'll never grow up."

"Good, young man, I'm very glad to meet you," Mr. Chai said. Indeed he hadn't expected that anyone younger than himself would know the great Russian poet by heart, but this young fellow from the countryside, though he looked like an oaf, could quote Yesenin off the top of his head. Mr. Chai was genuinely moved. He stretched out his hand, and they shook hands again.

Bin was afraid his host would talk more about Yesenin, so he fished the seal out of his army satchel. Carefully he opened the red paper and placed the green stone on the desk. He said to both Mr. Chai and his wife, "I came directly from your nephew's home and couldn't bring anything really artistic, so I carved this for you last night. I hope you like it. I'm so embarrassed to present you with such a trifle."

Mr. Chai picked up the seal, removed his glasses, and observed the engraving. Below his lower eyelids two purplish bags were quivering. Bin felt that Mr. Chai must have been knowledgeable about epigraphy, because he seemed to be examining the texture, suppleness, and vigor of the strokes.

Mr. Chai shook his head and chortled. "I'm damned again. You said you carved this last night?" he asked Bin.

"Yes. I had no time to paint or write calligraphy, so I carved this seal for you. I'm also a painter, you know."

"This is excellent work, young man!" Mr. Chai handed the seal to his wife and said, "Look at it, a real piece of art." Then he got to his feet and went to another room.

"See, you made him happy, Young Shao," Peina said, gazing at her husband's back while fingering the seal.

In no time Mr. Chai returned with a blank sheet of paper and a case of scarlet ink paste. He placed the sheet on a book and pressed the stone into the ink box. After blowing on the face of the seal, he stamped it on the paper. The square characters — YOUR BRUSH WRITES, RAISING WIND AND RAIN — appeared in a robust form. Mr. Chai bit his lower lip and said, "It's awesome, simply awesome. The lines are so ancient, so natural and sturdy. I'll stamp this on all my books."

Bin couldn't stop smiling and knew the Chais would surely help him.

Soon they were talking about the case over dinner, which was noodles with gravy made of minced pork and string beans. In addition, there were two side dishes: eggs stir-fried with leeks and a cucumber salad, seasoned with vinegar, mashed garlic, sesame butter, and a few tiny dried shrimp. Peina had received a long letter from her nephew a week before, so the Chais knew the whole story. She said it would be better if Bin himself took the written complaint to the editorial department the next morning. Bin was taken aback by the suggestion, suspecting she might not want to be too involved. She smiled and explained that her intention was to make the journal respond to the case in the coming issue, whose space had already been planned out. The only way to accomplish that goal was through touching the hearts of the editors, arousing their anger and sympathy, and convincing them of the necessity of reporting the case without delay. Mr. Chai told Bin to try to be emotional when he handed the letter of complaint to the editor in chief. It would be better if Bin could shed a few tears, because the sincerity of one's words could be gauged only by witnessing his emotion; words alone were merely clever creatures, which tended to arouse suspicion. But Bin must never appear glib in front of the editors. Mr. Chai didn't worry about that, since Bin looked pretty honest, even a little gauche.

As to Bin's lodging for the night, Mr. Chai suggested that he stay at a small inn outside the compound, because some of the editors, living in the same building as the Chais, would infer that Peina was involved in the case if they saw Bin enter or come out of her apartment. Then they wouldn't believe what Bin said at the editorial department the next day.

Bin thought Mr. Chai's suggestion was reasonable. So after tea, when the twilight turned indigo, Mr. Chai took Bin to the inn through the back door of the compound.

Walking along the sidewalk of a boulevard, under the fat sycamore leaves, he explained to Bin that he would have kept him company for another few hours, but two editors of *Law and Democracy* were coming to his home that night for a mah-jongg party at which they were going to discuss some publishing matters.

To make up for the early parting, Mr. Chai paid three yuan for Bin's lodging after telling the front-desk clerk that Bin was a friend of his and that they should give him a decent bed, which they managed to do.

At eight the next morning Bin arrived at the gray building that *Law and Democracy* shared with a bookstore. He climbed the creaking stairs to the top floor to see the editor in chief. To his surprise, the editorial department had only one large office. In the room four ceiling fans were languidly flapping their brass wings; about a dozen desks stood here and there; two khaki screens separated a few desks from the rest. A young woman with long hair over her sloping shoulders led Bin to the only mahogany desk, at which a dyspeptic-faced man, around forty, was sitting and writing on a pad of paper. Behind him, on the wall, spread a colorful map of China like a giant rooster.

"Here's Editor in Chief Wang," the woman said to Bin and turned away, back to the reception desk. Bin noticed that Peina was reading at a desk twenty feet away. She kept her head low but threw glances in his direction now and then.

"I'm Wang Min," the editor said, holding out his hand indifferently.

Bin gave his fleshy hand a shake. The second he sat down, he cleared his throat and began to speak. "My name is Shao Bin. I'm a worker and artist, from Gold County, Liaoning Province. I'm thirty-two, born in the Dog Year. I came to the capital to present a petition to you and hope you will help me and my comrades. I believe this is the place to look for justice." He paused, pulled a large envelope from his satchel, and presented it with both hands to the editor in chief.

Wang took the letter of complaint out of the envelope without removing his bleary eyes from Bin's face. He was a little puzzled by Bin's expression, which was between smiling and weeping. Tears were flickering in Bin's eyes and a few running down his cheeks. Wang couldn't tell whether Bin was too excited or too upset; he wondered why tears were shed so easily. He lowered his head and glanced through the first two pages of the complaint, then put it on the desk and asked Bin to talk about his case.

Bin went on, "I began to work as a fitter in Dismount Fort's Harvest Fertilizer Plant in 1971. I have worked well and studied conscientiously. Although I have only eight years' formal education, I taught myself painting, calligraphy, epigraphy, and poetry. The fine arts are my only hobby — no, my life. Up to now I have published about a hundred pieces of artwork in newspapers and magazines. To put it immodestly, I was the best-known man in our town. Because of my ability and name, some people in the plant are jealous of me."

He took a gray handkerchief out of his trouser pocket, blew his nose, and mopped his face. He let out a sob, then went on, "Last winter I published a cartoon in the *Lüda Daily* criticizing the unhealthy tendency in society, particularly about housing assignments. After the plant's leaders saw it in the newspaper, the Party secretary, Liu Shu, and the director, Ma Gong, began persecuting me. They called me a 'lunatic' at a general staff meeting and had my half year's bonus deducted. They said I had slung mud on the plant's face. From then on, they've seized every opportunity to oppress me. They beat me in their office and kicked my private parts at a conference. My entire family has suffered from their abuse of power."

He had to stop to catch his breath, since his sobbing had grown uncontrollable. A few of the editorial staff came over to listen to his story. Among them, of course, was Peina.

Bin continued to talk while tears streamed down his cheeks. Never had he been so heartbroken and so full of misery, as though a tap in him were broken and nothing could stop the fountains flowing down his face.

While he was talking about the leaders' evil deeds, all the misfortunes that had happened to him in the past arose in his mind: the hunger in the early 1960s, when he often cried for a genuine corn cake because everybody in the family had to eat wild herbs and elm bark; the death of his mother, drowned in a flood; his right leg broken in a sandpit in elementary school (for that, he was rejected by the drafting center and couldn't fulfill the ideal of his youth — to become a colonel or a general, a man well versed in both arms and letters); his having to repeat the fourth grade because he had flunked math; the two hundred yuan, half of the Shaos' savings, stolen from his pocket when he visited Shenyang City to see an art exhibition; his elder brother blown to pieces by a land mine in a militia drill; the death of his firstborn, a boy — a loss that had cut his family line . . .

Oh, life was an ocean of misery. There was no way to get out of the suffering except death. But he couldn't do that, not because he was a coward but because he had to take care of his family. It took more courage to live than to die.

His sobbing grew louder and louder and gradually turned into wailing, and his words became unclear. Nonetheless, the emotion he showed was so powerful that the good souls around him were deeply touched. One short young man poured a cup of black tea for Bin; the slim receptionist couldn't control her tears and wiped her eyes with pink toilet tissue. Though no longer able to speak coherently, Bin was absolutely fantastic, making the entire editorial staff gather around him, sighing and cursing the petty bureaucrats, and eventually he moved several women and an old man to weep with him. Intuitively Bin knew these were good people and would help him; they were able to weep simply because he, a stranger, was weeping painfully. Their hearts were pure and generous.

At last the editor in chief stood up and walked around the desk. "Comrade Shao Bin," he said amiably, placing his hand on Bin's shoulder, "please don't be too emotional. It will hurt your health. I promise that we'll study your material carefully and respond to it as soon as possible."

"Yes, we will help you," a few voices said in unison.

Bin tried to stop weeping and smile some. Their words soothed his scorched heart like a gurgling spring. Not until now did he remember that he had been putting on a show. Somehow he had lost himself altogether in the performance and had unconsciously entered into the realm of self-oblivion — a complete union with a character or an object, which he realized was the ideal state of artistic achievement, dwelled upon by many ancient masters throughout the history of Chinese arts. Again true artistic spirit had taken him unawares.

Still dazed by his emotional intensity, Bin managed to rise to his feet and picked up the army satchel. His handkerchief fell on the floor.

"Thank you, my good comrade," he mumbled, holding out his hand to Mr. Wang, who took it into his own. Bin said, "We're all looking forward to hearing from you.

I'll tell the folks in the countryside that the leaders and comrades in Beijing are upright and honest, and they've promised to help us restore justice."

"Yes, we will," Peina put in.

Bin touched the envelope on the desk and said to the editor in chief, "All the evidence and material you need are in this. Thanks, thanks." He turned to shake hands with several other men and women, then moved to the door and waved good-bye.

Peina picked up the handkerchief from under the chair and said, "He dropped this." She followed Bin out, crying loudly, "Comrade, wait a minute."

Once in the stairwell, she whispered to him excitedly, "You're great. It was spectacular! You should study the performing arts; I'm sure you'd become a movie star someday. Anyway, tell my nephew everything is all right and I'll try my best."

"Thank you, I will." Bin smiled, his temples still pounding.

They shook hands. Peina said, "I must go now. Good-bye." She turned back to the office.

It was past ten. Bin took a bus directly to the train station. The bus reeked of sweat, soap, toothpaste, cologne, medicinal herbs. So many passengers crowded into it that Bin soon found himself huffing and puffing. This must have been caused also by the female bodies pressing around him, especially that of a tall young woman from behind. She looked like a college student and a basketball player, with bobbed hair and a tanned face. Her hips in jeans rubbed the small of Bin's back as the bus jolted along. Bin's heart began galloping, though the bus was crawling like an oxcart. He thought he wouldn't mind riding this way for an hour or two, receiving this special massage.

But gradually his mind wandered in another direction. He imagined that this bus, so jam-packed, could be a vivid illustration of the concept of saturation, which he had learned from the chemistry textbook he had studied briefly three months before: If one more person squeezed in from the front door of the bus, a passenger on the bus would surely fall out of its rear door. Yes, this was saturation, a good human example.

In spite of the frantic traffic, Bin was longing to visit the Great Wall, the Forbidden City (which was said to have housed a lot of famous paintings), the Revolutionary Museum, the Summer Palace, and Chairman Mao's Mausoleum in Tiananmen Square, which had recently opened to the public. But he had to hurry back home, since his friends were anxiously awaiting him. He was to take the earliest train back to Gold County.

Fourteen

Seeing her husband back, Meilan shed joyful tears and said she had been afraid that Secretary Yang might have had him apprehended or assassinated in the capital.

What a bizarre idea, Bin thought. Even if Yang lorded over this commune and his flunkies could do whatever they liked here, they could hardly find their bearings in Beijing, to say nothing of abducting others. Yet Meilan's fear proved her love for him, so he was pleased.

Though having planned to go to work that morning, Bin was so exhausted that he soon fell asleep. His wife didn't wake him when she left for work; he snored nonstop for five hours.

Toward noon, when he woke, a note from Secretary Liu was lying beside him, saying that if Bin had been struck by diarrhea, as the medical certificate indicated, he should have been bedridden, unable to fool around in the county town, fanning up evil winds. Apparently he was well and didn't have to go to the latrine incessantly, so Liu ordered him to show up at work without delay.

Bin was too sleepy to worry about the note, which was dated the day before. He resumed snoring, his palm on his daughter's pillow.

During her lunch break, Meilan came back and cooked for Bin. Tired out, he didn't want to eat the dough-drop soup, and he told her he had to go to the plant.

Before leaving, he let her do cupping on him. She smeared a few drops of cold water on the hollow below his Adam's apple, lighted a scrap of paper with a match, dropped the fire into an empty jam jar, and pressed the "cup" tightly on the wet spot. In a few seconds a swelling rose inside the jar. He gave her a toothy grin, hoping she hadn't burned him.

"It's bloody dark," she said, referring to the swelling.

He couldn't speak, because the jar tightened his throat. He nodded at her twice.

After the cupping, he pulled on a low-necked T-shirt, so that the round patch on his throat was fully visible, like a gigantic birthmark. This would convince others of his illness, if not the leaders, who would turn a blind eye to his condition anyway. Examining the purple patch with a pocket mirror, Bin believed the treatment was timely. He obviously had too much poisonous fire in him and needed it to be sucked out. He put away the mirror and set off for the plant.

When Bin arrived at Maintenance, Hsiao greeted him,

waving a pair of greasy gloves, and told him bluntly, "The leaders think the medical certificate is a fake. They want to have these days deducted from your wages." Hsiao's tone, however, wavered as he noticed Bin's sick face and the dark patch on his throat.

Anger surged in Bin, but he didn't show it. He merely said, "Damn their mothers."

Hsiao assigned him to go to the lab and repair a ventilator. On his way there, Bin was wondering whether he should drop in on the leaders. For the three days' absence he might lose a little more than four yuan, but he needed the money badly, since he had already made up his mind to repay Jiang Ping for the fare. Besides, the deduction would hurt his name; he couldn't afford to let the whole plant think of him as a malingerer. He was certain that the leaders would publicize this and make his illness look like it came from mental or moral deterioration. There was also a strategic concern here. He was unsure whether or not the leaders knew of his trip; therefore he felt he should go and find out. Without entering a tiger's den, one couldn't catch tiger cubs. Yes, he ought to meet them.

Before he turned to the office building, Bin saw Secretary Liu coming out of the garage, with an umbrella under his arm. So Bin went up to him and asked why the leaders refused to acknowledge the sick-leave certificate. Liu said there was no Doctor Sun in the County Central Hospital and Bin had made up the whole thing.

"What?" Bin cried. "You have called the hospital to check on it, haven't you?"

"It's unnecessary." Liu waved his hand as though chasing a mosquito. "I tell you what, people here don't go to the Central Hospital for a sick-leave note. If you were really sick, you wouldn't have been able to move around in the county town. Now, tell me what you did there. Why didn't you stay in bed at home? You must confess everything first."

"I'll answer that after you tell me whether you're positive there's no Doctor Sun in the hospital. If you haven't checked, you'd better shut up."

Liu was taken aback by Bin's sharp tone of voice. "All right, describe to me what he looks like," he said and closed his eyes, ready to visualize Doctor Sun.

Bin's face went blank because he had never met the doctor; his nose was twitching while his mouth spread sideways.

Staring at Bin, Liu chuckled and said, "You aren't good at anything, you're not even a good liar. Go home and write out a confession of what you've been doing these days. Not until —"

"Damn it!" Bin cried, his senses restored at last. "Doctor Sun has big, dark eyes. I didn't see his face because he had on a large gauze mask. You must call the hospital and talk with him personally." Bin supposed Doctor Sun's eyes were similar to his nephew Song's.

Liu stopped chuckling and shifted his weight to the left leg. He said, "Okay, write out your confession and we may give you the pay."

"You give me the pay? This plant doesn't belong to you. It's our country's. The pay is given to me by the Party and the people. You have no right to take it away from me. I was sick and had diarrhea, couldn't move. No, I have nothing to confess."

"Then I can't help you."

"If you take a fen off my pay, my wife and I will visit your home every evening." Bin turned and walked away with a gleeful face.

For a whole day Bin's ears echoes with Tu Fu's lines inscribed on a painting of a grand eagle:

> When will it strike ordinary birds,
> Splattering blood and feathers on the plain?

Time and again, a large eagle emerged in his mind's eye, circling in the sky and catching sparrows, jays, swallows, titmice. The air was full of ecstatic cries and pitiful noises.

The poetry reminded him of the book of bird paintings published by Master Chen Fan, a distinguished professor in the Central Academy of Fine Arts in Beijing. Bin usually copied the book once a year as a part of his apprenticeship, but he had not done it for two years.

After supper, he moved to his corner in the room and

prepared to practice eagle painting. Meilan was listening to the historical serial *The Female Generals of the Yang Clan,* broadcast by Radio Liaoning, while Shanshan was playing with pocket magnifying glass on the floor. Bin spread out a large sheet of paper, opened the model book, and began to apply the brush.

For some reason he felt his wrist stiffen; the brush wandered without any sense of destiny. The eagle's broad wings turned out disproportionate, too large for its body and lacking the spirit of the model painting. He tore the sheet and threw it into the basket for kindling. He painted another piece, which came out similarly; the eagle's neck stretched up, like a giraffe's.

Bin was bewildered by the sudden change and thought it must have been caused by the noise from the radio. He wanted to tell Meilan to turn it off, but seeing her so engrossed in the Chinese troops pressing their attack against the northern barbarians, he changed his mind. Putting away the model paintings, he began to practice calligraphy by copying a stone rubbing. To his dismay, the brush seemed to have its own will, determined to disobey its master. The strokes on the paper lacked the vigorous movement of swords and spears, and a few even stretched like bands of black cloth waving in the breeze. Every word was devoid of life; some didn't stand upright and looked like piles of sticks. The characters just lay dead on the paper. Bin gave a sigh and put down the brush.

With his head hanging, he tried to think why all of a

sudden he couldn't harness the brush any longer. He felt as though something blocked his windpipe. One obvious cause of the relapse could have been that he hadn't worked hard on his arts these months but had spent too much time fighting those thugs. His heart was aching when a short poem on the methodology of study by a well-beloved octogenarian revolutionary echoed in his ears:

> Against the current you must punt hard;
> One stroke skipped, you fall back many a yard.
> The ancients said every minute was gold;
> So, cherish your time and have it controlled.

As though the poem triggered his lachrymal glands, all at once his face was flooded with tears. How he regretted wasting his time on those hoodlums! Why couldn't he concentrate on the real work and forget the turmoil outside? What good was getting the better of those idiots, who shouldn't have existed for him in the first place? Why couldn't he utilize his talent and energy exclusively for the improvement of his arts? For whatever reason, he should never have let his brushwork regress.

Shanshan noticed her father's tears and sang out, "Mommy, Daddy's crying again."

Meilan came over and patted him on the shoulder. "What's wrong?" she asked.

"My brush, oh, my brush becomes disobedient!" he wailed, rubbing his chest with both hands.

His wife broke out giggling, and Shanshan followed her mother, laughing too. Bin gazed at them, his face dark and long.

Meilan said to him, "I thought heaven collapsed or your mistress dropped dead. You scared us."

"What's so funny? I'm losing my mastery, my artistic power. Don't you see it?" He slapped the sheet of poor calligraphy on the desk.

"Stop talking like that." She didn't look at the characters. Instead, she took a towel and wiped the saliva off Shanshan's mouth. "You just had a bad day. Keep practicing. Nothing is as easy as eating noodles."

Somehow her casual remark enlightened him. Indeed this may be just a bad day, he thought. Probably it's only a painter's block. No artistic pursuit can be smooth sailing. It's a lifelong endeavor, and I mustn't lose heart so easily just because of temporary regression. I must persevere.

He struck a match, lighted a cigarette, and blew out a coil of smoke.

On payday Bin received his full wages. He took this as an initial victory. "If they gave me a fen less, I would shake heaven and earth," he told his fellow workers. Everybody was impressed, but some people still believed Bin had faked the sick-leave certificate. "Even the devil can be intimidated by a vile man," they said behind his back.

In fact the leaders were not frightened by Bin exactly, though they had called the County Central Hospital and spoken to Doctor Sun, who assured him that the sick-leave certificate was as genuine as their fertilizers. They were lenient to Bin this time for another reason. Three days ago they had received a classified bulletin which reported a tragedy that had resulted from a wage-scale adjustment. An old worker in Forever New Leather Mill in Sand County had lost his mind because most of his comrades had got a raise but he hadn't. To vent his rage on the mill's leaders, he blew up a corner of the apartment building where their families lived. Though nobody was killed, four people were seriously injured. Fortunately the old worker hadn't had access to TNT and had made do with a gunpowder package.

Unlike the leather mill, the Dismount Fort plant's Fourth Workshop produced high explosives for the army. Dynamite was always available to the workers here; quite a few men fished with homemade bombs; the year before last, an old storekeeper had been sentenced to eight years because he had in secret sold half a ton of TNT to a quarry and pocketed the cash. No doubt to Liu and Ma, Bin was insane and capable of doing anything, not to mention razing a house in Workers' Park. The bulletin gave full rein to their imagination, so they revoked the order to have three days' pay deducted from Bin's wages.

Fifteen

THREE WEEKS LATER an article about the case, entitled "Engulfed by the Evil Stream," came out in *Law and Democracy*. On his first reading of it, Bin was rather disappointed. The view and the tone of the writing were fine, but the report was too short, merely one and a half pages; the limited space wouldn't impress the reader. To Bin's mind, such an article should have been massive.

After reading it for the second time, though, he felt better and found it actually well written, even fiercely elegant. In fact, none of the main events and figures was left out. Reading it for the third time, he was impressed by the skill of the writer, who hadn't wasted a word, as though doing a poet's job.

His friends in Gold County were very pleased with the article. Yen called and said excitedly, "Brother Shao, this time we nabbed them. The County Administration wanted to talk with Old Jiang yesterday evening. Boy, they're scared."

"Good," said Bin.

Yen went on, "It's a victory, and they'll have to rehabilitate every one of us soon. Get ready for it, Brother. Don't let them off the hook easily."

Secretary Yang was shaken by the article and became restless. Intuitively he realized the whole thing would grow bigger and bigger if he didn't take action to stop it. The article's last sentence said clearly, "We are waiting with our eyes open to see how the local leaders will respond to this report." So he had to correct the case in time, to prevent the highest authority in the capital from pursuing him further.

His aide, Dong Cai, reported that Chairman Ding had ordered his men to investigate the case and interview Bin. Surely the enemy faction would use this article to destroy Yang, driving him out of Dismount Fort.

After brief consideration, Yang concluded that Bin was the key figure in the series of events. If he could pacify Bin, the Ding faction would be automatically stopped. By now he was very impressed by Bin's ability — not only as an artist but also as a political activist. Nobody else in the entire commune was able to get the attention of all levels of authorities and have his case printed in such a top legal journal. Eight months before, when he had read the report on Bin sent over by the fertilizer plant, Yang had thought Bin was no more than a crazed bookworm, of whom he had met many and had known how to handle them. Now he deeply regretted having neglected the talent in this small man.

In reality, Yang's faction was not as strong as Ding's, mainly because Chairman Ding had in his hands most of the writers in the commune and could maneuver without impediment in the field of propaganda. Yet Yang bet none of those pens in Ding's faction was as capable as Shao Bin, who could place articles and works of art in big newspapers and magazines with such ease. If only he had enlisted Bin's help.

He telephoned the Commune Guesthouse to have two dinners arranged. Then he had Dong Cai come in and told him to find Bin and take him to the guesthouse in the evening.

The first dinner started at three in the afternoon, in honor of the fertilizer plant's leaders. Two days before, Liu and Ma had read the article and got angry as usual, but they hadn't taken it as something that would cause any change. Bin remained the same maniac to them, and they wouldn't try to "rectify their mistakes" as the article demanded. By now they were somewhat used to this kind of warning from the media, which had always come like lightning without a storm.

The spacious dining hall in the guesthouse was empty, with all the chairs propped upside down on the tables. The terrazzo floor was wet and sprinkled with sawdust, which made the room smell of pine and cypress. Behind a set of sky blue screens on which white cranes were on the wing, the three diners — Yang, Liu, and Ma — sat down at a table covered with a green plastic tablecloth. They were going to eat prawn soup, crabs, and steamed buns stuffed with brown sugar.

"Since you both have read the article, what do you think we should do?" Yang asked.

"Believe me, Secretary Yang," said Ma, "Shao Bin is a mere lunatic. We should send him to a mental home."

Liu chimed in, "Yes, that will solve the problem once and for all. We're just fed up with him. He enjoys pestering others so much. Do you know what his nickname is in our plant?

"What?"

"Man Hater."

"We should have him locked up," Ma insisted.

"No, no." Yang shook his head, chuckling. "He isn't a lunatic. Even if he was, the whole of China knows of the case now, and we couldn't punish him without hurting ourselves."

The soup came in a white enamel basin, and the crabs and the sugar buns in two bamboo baskets. Liu and Ma remained silent, drinking brandy in gulps.

After the waitresses left, Yang resumed, "I'm positive Shao Bin is an able man. We must stop him; otherwise we'll all lose our jobs, or at least be demoted. The whole boat is in danger now. Chairman Ding will surely use this case to root us out. They're already on the move."

Both Liu and Ma were shocked, but they had no idea what to do, so they kept sucking crab claws.

Yang went on, "Ever since the ancient times, there have been two ways to get out of such a situation. One is punishment, the other is reward." He paused to take a spoonful of soup.

Seeing Liu's surprised look, Yang smiled and said, "Don't panic. I've decided to use reward. I'm going to be generous to Shao Bin. This is the only way to appease him now. Besides, I want to use him and make him our man, to keep him in our pond. But I'll have to punish you two in appearance. You'll be criticized in the internal bulletin. Don't be upset. Next year, I promise, you each will get a raise."

Yang went on explaining how he would reward Bin. Though both Liu and Ma thought Yang took the maniac too seriously, they were pleased that the secretary would take Bin into his own hands. From now on, they would be able to do many things in the plant without being painted and written about. As long as there was no disciplinary action against them, their official careers would be safe. Criticism in the internal bulletin would at most inflict a scratch on them, and people would forget it in a month. So without delay they praised Secretary Yang's wise, timely decision.

Before he left for the dinner, Bin whispered to Meilan in the corridor that if he didn't return that night, she mustn't go to the plant or the Commune Administration to look for him. Instead, she should get in touch with Yen, either by telephone or by telegram, and ask him to take emergency measures to get him out. Seeing that she was horrified by his words, he grinned and assured her that the invitation might be a reconciliatory sign from Yang. He then set off with Dong Cai, who had come to escort him to the Commune Guesthouse.

At the sight of Bin, Secretary Yang stood up and came across the dining hall to meet him. Holding Bin's hand, he said, "I'm sorry, Comrade Young Shao. I was at a meeting just now and couldn't go to your home to invite you in person." He smiled amiably, the mole on his nose quivering like a bee.

The warmth Yang showed put Bin at ease instantly, though Bin still couldn't fathom what this meant. The dishes on the green tablecloth looked so appetizing, especially the pair of smoked yellow croakers and the braised pork cheek that had been sliced and arranged into a large lotus.

"Sit here," Dong said to Bin, pulling a chair closer to the table.

As soon as they sat down Yang raised a glass of Jade Spring wine and proposed a toast, "To your glorious future, Young Shao."

Following Yang and Dong, Bin took a sip, weighing the word *glorious.* He couldn't help wondering whether there was poison in the red wine and regretted having drunk it. But he curbed his fantasy, telling himself that they dared not poison him so soon. He put down the glass carefully as Yang pointed his chopsticks at the dishes, saying, "Please help yourself."

Though still baffled, Bin ate a piece of the smoked fish Dong had put on his plate. Then Yang began to apologize for interceding for him so late, but he swore by his Party member's conscience that he hadn't been involved in persecuting him, that there was a lot of misunderstanding between them, and that he had reprimanded the plant's leaders. Bin thought Yang was scared. Damn you, he said in his mind, you also have fearful moments. It's too late to extricate yourself.

"Comrade Shao Bin," Yang said, chewing a pine mushroom, "I know you're an artist and a learned scholar. To take advantage of your knowledge and talent, I've decided to transfer you to the Commune Administration. Your rank will be the twenty-second, and you'll have your own office and do propaganda work." Yang smiled, observing Bin's eyes blinking at him. He went on, "You shouldn't remain in the fertilizer plant and waste your talent like this. I hope you accept my offer."

"Yes, I do, I do." Bin sounded beside himself, and he lifted the glass and drained it to conceal his excitement.

Immediately Dong refilled the glass. With his two gold teeth glittering in the fluorescent light, Dong said, "Congratulations, Young Shao. Welcome to our team."

"Thanks."

"But there're two small things I'd like you to do," Yang said. "Number one, you should stop fighting with Liu Shu and Ma Gong. You and they are all revolutionary comrades and will be colleagues; you shouldn't waste your energy and time this way. We live in the same water and can't snap at each other all the time. In a word, save your energy to fight our enemy. Number two, if you're satisfied with the job transfer, please write a short letter to the editors of *Law and Democracy* and tell them our Commune Administration has corrected the mistake and you are satisfied with the result."

Neither of the demands seemed hard to meet. Both Ma and Liu were of the twenty-first rank, but they wouldn't dare offend Bin anymore, because he was going to work above them at the Commune Administration. Besides, he had friends in the county town now. Without thinking further, Bin said, "I will do both."

Yang smiled and proposed another toast.

Dong Cai began talking to Bin about the advantages of working at the Commune Administration, especially under the leadership of Secretary Yang; but Bin ought to be careful when dealing with Chairman Ding and the people close to Ding, particularly Tian Biao, the director of the General Affairs Section.

The yellow croakers were fresh and crispy, and within half an hour Dong and Bin had almost finished the pair of big fish; Secretary Yang didn't eat much and only drank the wine. Bin couldn't help wondering who the chef was who could cook such a delicious dish, but he didn't ask. He would find this out by himself.

Overwhelmed by the promotion, Bin couldn't help smiling and nodding to Yang and Dong again and again. He kept doing this until Yang said he had another meeting to attend and proposed the last toast. "To our solidarity," he said. They clinked glasses and drank up.

To Yang's amazement, Bin stood up, almost in tears, and said, "Secretary Yang, the ancients said, 'A virtuous man should die for the lord who appreciates him, just as a good woman should dress up for the man who loves her.' Trust me, I will work hard and live up to your expectations."

Yang was very pleased and impressed by Bin's sense of loyalty. With the tip of his tongue wiping his oily lips, he said, "Good, Young Shao, I trust you. Our propaganda work will depend on you."

Before Bin left, Yang told him to get ready to start as soon as possible, since there was a lot of writing and painting to do at the administration.

* * *

After Bin told Meilan of Yang's offer, her face fell, and a few dark wrinkles appeared on her forehead. "Did you accept it?" she said.

"Of course," he answered.

She didn't ask further. She got up from the chair and went out to cook dinner for herself and Shanshan. Within seconds the ladle and the wok began clattering peevishly. Realizing she was unhappy about the offer, he went out, held her bony wrist, and dragged her back into the room.

"What's wrong?" he asked.

"You only think of yourself and never have us in mind."

"What makes you say that?"

"You only care about your own promotion. Where are we going to live? Still in this room?" She shook his hand off, picked up a dishrag, and went out again.

Her words struck him dumb. Obviously his head had been turned by a half victory. Why on earth had he forgotten to ask for housing? He shouldn't have let them buy him off so easily. Now what should he do?

He went out into the corridor again, trying to comfort Meilan by saying he would think out a plan to ensure that they would have an apartment. But in his heart he had no idea what to do.

The next morning he went to the post office and called *Environment.* Yen answered the phone. He told Bin that there had also been a breakthrough in Gold County: The newspaper would restart the next week and the bureau's leaders agreed to increase its annual budget by twenty percent. After hearing of the new development in Dismount Fort, Yen invited Bin to a banquet at his home. He explained, "It's not my own idea. Jiang and Song want to celebrate too. Please join us at five Friday afternoon."

"What should I bring?" asked Bin.

"Nothing but your stomach."

Bin promised he would come; then he mentioned the housing problem and asked Yen how he should resolve it. Yen said, "Bin, don't rush. If they've bought a horse, of course they have a saddle for it. Once you become a cadre, you'll automatically have housing. It's only a matter of time. If I were you, I wouldn't make a request now."

The more Bin thought about Yen's words, the more sense they made. An immediate request might give Secretary Yang the impression that he was too materialistic, haggling before doing any work.

For a whole day Bin kept reminding himself: You must rise with temperance. And he felt grateful to Yen, who was so knowledgeable about official life and always ready to help him.

But Meilan wasn't easy to persuade. In the evening, when Bin explained Yen's advice to her, she said loudly, "We've lived in this pigpen too long! I can't stand it anymore."

"Come on, just wait a year or two, all right? Every

cadre at the Commune Administration has a good place to live. Sooner or later they'll assign us an apartment."

"How soon? Another two years? I guess we'll be old when —"

"Okay, a few months."

"The truth is you are obsessed with the official position."

"No, I'm not doing this for myself. If I hold an important job, life will be easier for our family. Don't be silly. I don't want to give Yang Chen a bad impression when I start. You know the first impression is always indelible."

She lay down on the bed and covered her head with a blanket.

Ignoring her, he went about composing the letter he had promised Yang to send out. On a piece of official stationery, which he had saved for special letters, he wrote these words:

> The Most Respected Editor in Chief Wang:
>
> Although I left the capital several weeks ago, your instructive words still linger in my ears. Thank you for publishing the article, which helped the leaders of our commune realize and rectify the mistake immediately. Secretary Yang Chen had a heartwarming talk with me, and decided to transfer me to a position more suitable to my talent. This could not have happened without your timely intervention.
>
> I am informed that the Administration of Gold County has already reinstated the newspaper *Environ-*

ment, and that its editorial staff are all satisfied with the final settlement.

Thank you again, sincerely. Please give my warmest regards to your colleagues.

Loyally yours,
Shao Bin

P.S. Please print this letter in your journal.

He was certain that it would be printed, because there couldn't be a better way for the journal to display its clout and righteous spirit. The brushwork in the letter was offhand, so that the characters appeared rather graceful and cloudy.

Since Meilan didn't want to speak to him, Bin left without a word for the post office, with the letter in his pocket. He knew her temper well and was sure that in a day or two she would be herself again.

At seven-thirty the next morning, Bin set out for his new position. He carried a shiny attaché case that Liu and Ma had presented to him as a souvenir from the plant; in the case were a bunch of brushes, the ink slab, and a book of aphorisms by famous authors and scientists. His first task was to paint a mural at the thoroughfare in town, supporting the national campaign against bourgeois liberalization. The paints and ladders were all ready in his office; he was given two helpers, hefty young men, for the work.

On his way to the Commune Administration, he couldn't resist smiling and whistling. In the sky a flock of geese were drifting south and gradually merging into the cotton clouds. Joyously Bin stretched up his right arm, as if he too had wings.

ALSO BY HA JIN

OCEAN OF WORDS: STORIES

Winner of the PEN/Hemingway Award

The place is the chilly border between Russia and China. The time is the early 1970s when the two giants were poised on the brink of war. And the characters in this thrilling collection of stories are Chinese soldiers who must constantly scrutinize the enemy even as they themselves are watched for signs of the fatal disease of bourgeois liberalism.

In *Ocean of Words*, Ha Jin explores the predicament of these simple, barely literate men with breathtaking concision and humanity. From amorous telegraphers to a pugnacious militiaman, from an inscrutable Russian prisoner to an effeminate but enthusiastic recruit, Ha Jin's characters possess a depth and liveliness that suggest Isaac Babel's Cossacks and Tim O'Brien's GIs. *Ocean of Words* is a triumphant volume, poignant, hilarious, and harrowing.

"A compelling collection of stories, powerful in their unity of theme and rich in their diversity of styles."
—*The New York Times Book Review*

Fiction/Short Stories/0-375-70206-7

AVAILABLE FROM PANTHEON BOOKS
AND FORTHCOMING FROM
VINTAGE IN 2000

WAITING

Winner of the 1999 National Book Award for Fiction

0-375-40653-0 (cloth)
0-375-70641-0 (paper)

Vintage International
Available at your local bookstore, or call toll-free to order:
1-800-793-2665 (credit cards only).